ELIVA'S CHILD

LAURA ZIEGLER

Gratitude

So many people made this book possible that I could not possibly list them all! I hope you know who you are and how much your love and support has meant to me.

To my wonderful husband, Russell, my parents, Peter & Wendy, and my sister, Heather: Thank you for reading through the many, many drafts, helping me navigate some of the stickier scenes, and providing steadfast encouragement along the way.

To my editors, Ronan Sadler & Rawles Lumumba, and my graphic designer, Maggie Roberts: all I can say is WOW!

And finally, thank you to Princess Taliya, who has remained my faithful friend throughout this whole process, even if she occasionally wants to knock some better sense into me.

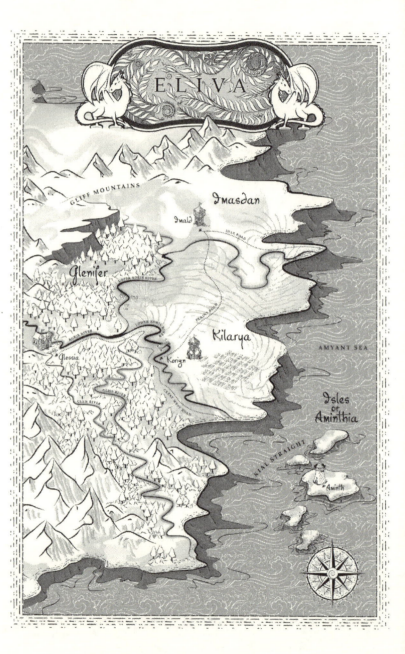

Prologue

Kellay glared at her husband, daring him to argue. He sighed and held out his hand to her. As he did, his sleeve slipped back to reveal traces of a tattoo snaking up his arm, marking him as Guardian. Kellay had a matching tattoo and her throat closed in anguish for what that mark meant today. Still, she relented to his silent request and grasped his hand with her own.

"I have served Him faithfully. I have done everything He has ever asked but He cannot—*cannot*—ask this of me!"

"Kellay, we must." Her husband's voice was hoarse.

"But what about the baby? The prophecy you interpreted clearly said only the eldest was the Chosen; it said nothing of the baby. How could He be so cruel as to take both our children at once? What is the price of sacrifice?"

"Kellay, hush. You saw the prophecy as well as I."

"Yes, I *know* the Other is coming into power."

Both of their children started to cry, and Eltang frowned at his wife and shook his head. Kellay heard the silent reprimand for upsetting their children. Every Guardian knew who the Other was from the moment they were born. The fear of the Other was as ingrained in them as their love for Mansra. That her youngest daughter was a baby still and her oldest one not yet four made no difference. Even the name of the Other spoken aloud would affect them deeply. "But so what if th- so what if *he* is coming into power? Should that give Mansra the right to take *our children?* Why can't I go instead?"

"Kellay, hush," Eltang said again. "We don't question Mansra. He is right, and He is good. If our children are called by Him, it is because they are needed to serve his purpose. The strength of the Guardians flows strongest in the veins of the young—you know that. We are too weak to take th- to take *him* on."

Kellay looked away from her husband. She knew that. It used to be that Mansra protected many worlds, but not any longer—not since the Other had stepped into the picture. As the Other's power grew, Mansra's faded. If the Other destroyed *Mansra,* then the worlds would be lost. That was why Kellay's children were being taken from her. Who else but the Guardians' firstborn would be strong enough to restore the balance? But…these were *her* children.

Kellay grabbed her husband's arm. She glanced at her eldest daughter, then switched her language to one of the ancient tongues—one that her daughter had not yet learned. Would never learn, now. Not if she was being taken off the Guardian planet.

"*You* know how they are taken. It's dangerous. So many children don't make it through. So many lives are lost…and if anyone finds out who they are…" Kellay choked on the words, and she suppressed a scream.

"We are Guardians, Kellay. There is a price to protecting the worlds."

"*They're* not Guardians. Not yet. They won't survive without His protection."

Kellay felt her husband's fingers tense around her own and looked up at him.

"I gave the eldest His ring."

Kellay glanced down at her eldest daughter's hands, restraining her desire to gather up both her children and flee before the priests came. She saw the ring, now that she knew to look for it. Mansra's ring had been entrusted to him when he had entered Guardianship. Kellay didn't question how her husband's ring fit her four-year-old perfectly. Once given, the ring would fit its new bearer. So it had always been.

"But you can't! That is not yours to give. He won't be pleased." Yet as she said this, Kellay felt hope swell in her heart.

Please, Mansra, Kellay prayed to Him, *let her never take the ring off. Let it protect them both.* She was so desperate she almost called

Him by name, but stopped herself in time. It was never wise for Guardians to invoke Mansra's true name. "We'll never see them again," Kellay said, defeated. "They'll be all alone out there."

"They have each other, love," her husband said. "Be strong, now."

"I am strong," Kellay snapped.

She was more than strong: she was Guardian. She looked to the door as the priests arrived.

1

"And you will know the end has come by these signs: the sun will blacken into darkness, creatures will come from the depths of the ground to destroy the people, and Elyan will rise up from the ashes of fire. Thus, will Eliva fall." –From the Prophecies of Berech

Deep underground, in a kingdom all but forgotten by humans, the drægonelle hissed uneasily. The human girl was awake again, and having visions. The drægonelle checked on her sleeping baby, then stretched her mind out, trying to *see* her. It was difficult, as the girl was not one of hers. Not yet, anyway. The drægonelle closed her midnight blue eyes and focused. It took a few minutes. At first all the drægonelle had were impressions: the rustle of a human dress whispering across the ground, the pounding heartbeat of the girl—she was frightened again. Frightened of her visions.

Her baby twitched, sensing her mother's tension, and the drægonelle paused to nuzzle her until she settled back into a dreamless sleep. She took an extra moment to stare in both wonder and dread at her baby, her daughter. The wonder was at the power that her daughter was growing into every day; the dread was in knowing that her own days were numbered. The prophecies had warned her that as the human girl came in to her full power as prophet of the end times, the drægonelle's days were numbered. Soon, she would have to go to the surface where she would meet her end, and all hope would be with her baby. Her baby, and the human girl whose distress had woken the drægonelle from her sleep.

The drægonelle snorted and blew out smoke in anguish. The prophecies about the end times were clear, but the drægonelle still held hope that the human girl and her daughter would find a loophole, a way to escape the destruction of their world. *She* hadn't found it after all her centuries of searching, but that didn't mean it wasn't there. Time was running short, and there was so much she needed to do before the end, but the closer that day came the more the drægonelle dreaded it. There was something wrong with the human girl that she watched; something that smelled almost of deceit. With each passing day, the taste of this deceit grew stronger in the drægonelle's mouth, but she did not know what it meant. All she knew was that it was wrong. When the girl arrived here, perhaps she would know. The drægonelle had already sent orders to the horses that lived in the palace with the girl; they knew to bring the girl here when they found opportunity to do so. She had been trying to reach the girl through her dreams, enticing her into the woods where they could meet. But the drægonelle's connection with humans wasn't as strong as with horses, and she would just have to be patient. She sighed at the irony. Already she had lived hundreds of years, and now when it mattered most she had no time.

The drægonelle cast her mind back to the girl, trying to reconnect with her. It was so difficult, so difficult when the humans did not belong to her. But this one would, she reminded herself. This one would, and then maybe she would understand what was *wrong* about her. She closed her eyes and focused. The girl was speaking in the highborn Kilaryan accent, and it took the drægonelle a few moments to remember the language so she could translate the words in her mind.

"It's me and it's *not* me. It's like…it's like there are two of me. It just doesn't make sense. Night after night I see myself dying in that fire. In one way, I'm barely more than a babe, but I'm also older…a young child, you know? But I've never even *been* trapped in a fire, so why such dreams? I wake up and can still feel it burning me. And then there is that blackness. That awful, hungry blackness that grabs me and swallows me up."

"Dreams are strange, Princess Taliya. They play trickster to us all." Jef smiled at his garden. "Lilies are simple flowers. They just grow where they're planted. A Princess's life is not so simple, eh?"

Princess Taliya smiled at the gardener. When the nightmares had first come, Princess Taliya had escaped the student dorms for the openness of the gardens. She hadn't spoken to Jef at first, other than to dismiss the gardener from her presence. Taliya was as polite to the servants as anyone else, but she didn't share her secrets with them. She didn't even share them with her best friend, Juliette.

Yet Jef had played a subtle game that had intrigued Taliya from the start. He didn't treat her with the same careful deference most of the servants adopted in her presence. But he *listened*. Before she knew it, she found herself telling him of her constant nightmares—nightmare, she corrected herself, since there was only one—that forced her to seek refuge in the gardens almost every morning. Under his gentle gaze, Taliya found herself wanting to confess her secrets aloud.

"Good night, Jef."

He cracked a wise smile at her. "Until the morrow, Princess."

Taliya rolled her eyes at him. "Goodness, I hope not!"

Jef bowed, and she turned on her heel. Her conversation with the gardener had left her feeling lighter, and Taliya skipped back to the gate, kicking at the dead leaves as she did so. She was just pulling open the door when her ring burned in warning and she ducked. An arrow planted itself above her head, and Taliya shrieked.

"Princess!" Jef cried, surging towards her. There was an answering shout from the walls above as one of the guards took up the cry. Footsteps echoed as people ran down the stone stairway at the edge of the gardens.

There was a *thump* as if something fell out of a tree, and a small boy broke out from the bush, carrying a bow that was almost as tall as he was. He wore the uniform of a fosterling.

"I'm sorry, I'm so sorry, I know I shouldn't have been practicing in here and I-"

He stopped dead when he saw her and collapsed to his knees. The bow dropped beside him, forgotten.

"I didn't mean it, I didn't mean it!" he wailed.

Guards surrounded the fosterling who looked even smaller in their presence. Taliya watched him shrink away from the guards and her heart squeezed.

On her sixth birthday, Lord Maddoux had given her a puppy. Taliya had instantly fallen in love with its big, brown eyes and shaggy brown fur. Within a few days Taliya's mother had the puppy removed, stating that it was too filthy to be around the princess. The puppy had cried when the queen's guard carried it away, and for weeks afterwards Taliya had nightmares about those whimpers of despair. She had screamed and cried and begged her mother to bring the puppy back, but her pleas fell on deaf ears. There was something in the boy's face that reminded her of that puppy. *But I'm not six years old any longer*, Taliya reminded herself. *I couldn't protect my puppy, but I can protect this fosterling.*

"Your Highness, what happened?" one of the guards asked. He held up a lantern to peer at her more closely, and his face darkened in anger.

"Send for Talon and Sorcerer Maddoux. They must know of this treachery."

The boy's eyes widened in terror. "But it wasn't- I didn't mean- I didn't-"

"What happened?" Taliya demanded.

"Your Highness, we should await testimony until Talon and Lord-"

Taliya gave him a look that silenced him. No matter that she was barely 15 years old, she was still their princess. "I have a right to question him."

The guard pressed his lips together, his eyes narrowing.

"Well, Fosterling?" Taliya prodded.

The boy looked up at her, tearful. "Please, my name's Bryndan...Fosterling Bryndan. I didn't *mean* to shoot at you.

Another boy was teasing me this morning, saying that I couldn't draw this bow if I tried. Said I would never be a knight. I told him he was wrong. He said *prove it*, so I told him-" Bryndan hiccoughed. "I told him that when he walked through the gardens on his way to training tomorrow there would be an arrow sticking in that wall," he gestured to a spot on the wall well above Taliya's head, "and he would know it was me, and that I could too draw this bow."

"Fosterlings are forbidden to use bows unsupervised, and *never* in the gardens," the guard said with a frown.

Bryndan hung his head.

"I just wanted to show him. If I had shot the arrow in the training grounds, he would have said that *anybody* could have shot that arrow."

"You climbed in the tree to get a better shot? Didn't you *see* me?" Taliya asked.

Bryndan swallowed.

"Honest, I thought you were well enough away."

Taliya sighed. She *had* been well enough away, right until she had skipped her way into the arrow's path.

She looked up at the high spot on the wall that Bryndan had indicated, then at the arrow planted at her eye level in the door. "I don't know whether to congratulate you for being a good shot or scold you for being a bad one," she mused.

Bryndan missed the humour in her voice and hung his head.

Jef looked at the wall, looked down at the arrow, and cleared his throat. Taliya wasn't sure if he was hiding a laugh or not. Knowing Jef, he was probably relieved the stray arrow had not struck any of his well-tended lilies, even if they had already been dead-headed for winter.

"Yes, my lady," Bryndan mumbled.

He looked so dejected that Taliya was about to offer him a word of comfort when the door burst open behind her. Talon—the Captain of the Guards who broke tradition when he earned his station by merit alone—was the first out the door. He paused to bow to her before approaching the scene.

"I'm glad to see you're okay, Highness."

"It was an accident, Talon." Taliya cautioned. "He's just a fosterling who needs training."

Talon sighed. "We still have to inform Lord Craelyn of this, and the boy will need to be questioned."

"You mean Sorcerer Maddoux, surely?" Taliya frowned.

Talon shrugged. "Sorcerer Maddoux is unwell. His apprentice, Lord Craelyn has been taking over all his duties."

Taliya's heart skipped a beat. Talon nodded to one of his guards, who grabbed Bryndan by the shoulder and hauled him inside. When the captain turned to go after him, Taliya caught his sleeve to hold him back. She glanced at Jef, who bowed and backed away. Once they were alone, Taliya lowered her voice.

"Sorcerer Maddoux...he'll pull through this one, right, Talon?"

"He took a turn for the worse yesterday." Talon hesitated. "It... doesn't look good, Princess. Even the greatest of wizards can't cheat death when it comes knocking."

Taliya gave a sharp nod, blinking to hide her tears.

"What will this do to my people? Sorcerer Maddoux means so much to them." *He means so much to* me.

Taliya didn't say those words aloud, but Talon reached out and squeezed her hands as if he had heard them, his eyes filled with compassion.

"Go to him, Princess. He would like that."

Taliya hesitated, then withdrew her hands. "Not yet. I need to attend to Fosterling Bryndan's trial first."

Talon's eyebrows raised.

"It was an *accident*, Talon, I know it was. He seems like such a sweet boy, and he doesn't deserve to be punished. Sorcerer Maddoux is the face of justice, but Lord Craelyn isn't...he isn't...the same."

Talon sighed. "You must learn to trust him, Taliya. Sorcerer Maddoux chose him as successor, and you must trust his judgement."

"Of course, I trust him," Taliya said hurriedly. "I just...he's so young. I feel I should see this through, to honour Sorcerer Maddoux."

Talon still looked puzzled, but he nodded and shrugged, withdrawing his hands. It was not for him to question the princess' decisions.

"I'll attend to Sorcerer Maddoux as soon as the trial is over."

"He would like that," Talon said softly. He bowed and headed inside, leaving Taliya alone in the garden.

Once he was gone, Taliya sank against the wall. She yawned and rubbed her eyes as the adrenaline of the night faded away, leaving her exhausted. Taliya glanced up at the sky, which was already lightening. The Council would meet immediately after morning bell to discuss these events. They would hear testimony from Lord Craelyn and then Bryndan, before deciding his fate. Taliya, as a member of the royal family, was not required to stand witness, but she would be permitted to speak her Voice in the Council if she requested so ahead of time. To get permission, she needed to speak with her parents immediately. She yawned again and then opened the garden door to head inside. She headed straight to her royal rooms. On the way, she caught the attention of one of the servants.

"Send Pallaster to my rooms at once."

The man bowed and strode quickly down one of the corridors.

Taliya got to her rooms and wasted no time searching for some suitable attire among her wardrobe. She couldn't wear her student's frock if she was going to be attending the Council today. Pallaster arrived a few moments later, with two maids trailing her. Her face had the pillow creases of someone who had just gotten out of bed, but her hair was in place and her frock neat. Taliya was always impressed with how quickly the handmaid put herself together on such short notice.

"Your Highness." Pallaster curtsied as she entered the room and the two maids did the same. The dark-haired one was familiar to Taliya, but the one with flaming red hair was new.

"Pallaster, I need to visit my parents today."

"Of course." She came alongside Taliya and began eyeing the different dresses. "On what sort of business?"

"A fosterling blundered an arrow earlier this morning and it nearly killed me. I need permission from my parents to speak in Council at his trial so I can defend him."

Pallaster raised an eyebrow. "*Defend* him, Highness?"

"It was an accident, Pallaster. I know it was. The poor boy is a terrible shot and I may have skipped my way in front of him at the wrong moment."

Pallaster giggled. "Oh, my! That's terrible. I'm so glad you're all right but oh, how *awkward* a mistake...from being a bad shot to attempting to assassinate the Crown Princess." Pallaster snorted and reached out to snag a light purple frock with gold trim.

"This one, Highness. It will bring out your lovely golden eyes and the lower cut will ensure anyone who sees you that you have not been harmed. At least, not in the bosom," Pallaster teased.

Taliya laughed. "Shame, Pallaster! I have no bosom to speak of."

One of the maids—the one with the dark hair—burst out laughing before quickly covering her mouth with her hand. The fiery-haired one remained expressionless as she assisted Pallaster.

With the help of Pallaster and her capable assistants, it wasn't long before Taliya's hair was combed into place, and she was dressed and ready to face her parents.

"All finished," Pallaster said with a curtsy.

It was shortly after dawn when Taliya approached the door to her parents' private chambers. The guard at the door nodded a greeting to her from his post.

She could hear her parents talking.

"-without Sorcerer Maddoux? What about the children?" The queen sounded worried.

Taliya's hand froze where it was, poised to knock on the door. She bit her lip.

"Lord Craelyn will know what to do. He *must* know what to do. We won't survive unless we-"

The guard at the door cleared his throat, raising his eyebrow at her eavesdropping, and Taliya flushed. She knocked quickly. Inside the room, her parents hushed.

"Enter," King Allandrex called.

Taliya walked in and shut the door behind her. She curtsied, discretely rubbing her sweaty palms on her dress as she did so.

"Taliya, child, praise Berech you're alright!" Allandrex kissed the top of her head.

"You look pale, sweetheart. Are you sleeping well enough?" Charlestte asked.

"Of course, mother." Taliya couldn't bring herself to tell them about the nightmares. They would send for a shyliac to see if she was sick, and then the whole palace would know all about her nightmares.

"I… I wanted to talk to you about what happened."

"Of course. Come sit with us."

Taliya sat, and Queen Charlestte cleared her throat meaningfully. When Taliya glanced over at her mother, the queen gestured for Taliya to sit straighter, which she did. Charlestte smiled.

"I don't believe the fosterling was trying to kill me. It was an accident. I wasn't paying attention to my surroundings and… well, it was just bad luck and bad aim on his part. I'm worried about his punishment."

"Sweetheart, he could have killed you with that arrow. He *must* be punished."

"I know. I just… I know it was an accident. He deserves the benefit of doubt."

"Taliya," Allandrex was frowning. "This is for the Council to decide."

"Then I request to give Voice at the Council."

The king rose to his feet, and Charlestte put a calming hand on his arm.

"How would it look if you were to defend him before the Council?"

"Like the truth!"

"Taliya," Charlestte chided, and Taliya snapped her mouth shut. She took a deep breath.

"Please, let me speak my testimony. It's permitted upon my request, and that's what I'm doing right now. I'm not trying to interfere with the Council's decision. I just want to make sure that the fosterling's punishment is a true reflection of his crime."

"Well, then." Charlestte said, standing up. Taliya followed suit. She could sense her dismissal. The queen glanced at her husband, who was still frowning.

Charlestte grabbed her hand and kissed Taliya's cheek. "You're growing up." She smiled.

Taliya's heart filled with hope. "I have your permission?"

"Yes, dear, you do. Now off to morning meal with you."

Taliya hesitated.

"Mother?" she asked. "Is it true that Sorcerer Maddoux is dying?"

Charlestte sighed. "It is," she said.

"What will this mean for us?" *What did you mean about the children?* Taliya wanted to ask, but she couldn't bring herself to admit she had been eavesdropping.

Charlestte rose and clasped her hands, much in the same way that Talon had. Allandrex came over and kissed her on her forehead.

"It means a great sadness for all of us, but nothing will change. Lord Craelyn is said to be even more powerful than Sorcerer Maddoux. He will protect us in the times ahead."

"What times ahead?"

The queen glanced at her husband, who shook his head slightly. "Never mind, Taliya. Everything will be fine. We'll see you at Council."

2

"Let no man know no justice." – Kilaryan proverb

Taliya's hands shook slightly when she was called in as witness before Council. She had been waiting impatiently outside the chambers for hours now, and she wondered how Bryndan was holding up. She glanced over at him as she walked over to the witness stand. He looked small and defeated as he sat shivering in a chair before the Council. Talon stood beside him with one hand on his shoulder. Taliya hadn't thought Talon would attend Bryndan's trial, but she supposed he was there to make sure Bryndan remained calm and contained.

"-weak, but his heart is true and his family has always been loyal to the crown."

"He is not a true Kilaryan," Lord Craelyn said. "We cannot attest to the loyalty of a foreigner."

Taliya's heart sank. She had hoped Lord Craelyn would be on Bryndan's side.

Lord Jeo turned to the assistant sorcerer. "His mother immigrated from Glenifer when she was a child. I hardly think that qualifies him as a 'foreigner'."

"No Gleniferite can be trusted! One only has to look at their backwards ideology to know—"

From the Council chairs, Allandrex cleared his throat. Lord Craelyn quickly bowed to the Council.

Lord Kade, the Council mediator (and Taliya's uncle), spoke. "Glenifer is not on trial here, Lord Craelyn. Nor does Council judge a man—or boy—by his heritage. It is the fosterling's *actions* that we are here to discuss."

Lord Jeo grunted. "And I remind Council that the fosterlings are *my* responsibility. I ask Council to consider my request to let *me* sort out this fosterling's punishment. He is a fool, and a weakling… but if he's a killer I would lay on my own sword."

"Thank you for your testimony, Lord Jeo," Lord Kade said. "Even though we don't need such dramatic pronouncements."

Lord Jeo bowed to the Council. He turned and hesitated when he saw Taliya. The training master approached her and bowed over her hand.

"Apologies if there was any insult, Your Highness, but I meant every word," he murmured, too quietly for Council to hear.

When he looked back up at her, Taliya smiled and nodded to show her support. Lord Jeo gave a small nod back and then stood upright. She thought Lord Jeo would leave immediately, but the training master took up a guard stance on the other side of Bryndan, next to Talon. He must have been acting as Bryndan's guardian then, since his parents were not present.

"Princess Taliya, here to give witness," Lord Kade announced. The Council mediator was a renowned historian and an expert on Kilaryan laws, but his teaching skills were lacking, and Taliya found his history classes rather boring.

Taliya curtsied to the Council. Seated with them she saw her cousins—Milahny and Erok—and swallowed her jealousy. The children of her father's younger brother, Lord Kade, they had joined the Council a few years ago, when they had been Taliya's age. Perfect Milahny, who was second in line for the throne after Taliya, could only be described as sugar mixed with sunshine. Taliya loved her cousin, but Milahny always made Taliya feel awkward and ugly. That Milahny never intended to make Taliya feel that way only made her feel worse.

"My lords and ladies," Taliya said formally. "Thank you for allowing me to share my testimony."

As Taliya described the events of the night—skipping vaguely over her reasons for being in the garden at that time—she tried not to pay attention to Lord Craelyn on her left, who was watching her closely. The apprentice sorcerer's fingers drummed absently against his thighs as he watched her.

"So you see, the gardener Jef and I could both attest that—by all appearances—it *was* an accident and poor timing on my part for jumping in the path of the arrow."

"The servant has no voice at Council, and you are not permitted to speak for him," Lord Kade warned. Taliya curtsied an apology. She knew that, but it didn't hurt to remind the Council that there was more than one witness to the event, even if one of those witnesses didn't count.

"I have a few questions for our witness," Craelyn said to the Council. Allandrex frowned, but he nodded.

"Princess Taliya, you were a bit vague as to what you were doing out in the gardens so late at night… and with a *gardener* no less."

Taliya frowned. "As I said, I couldn't sleep and thought a walk in the fresh air would do me some good."

"And you just… walked into this gardener and started talking?" Craelyn's brow furrowed in confusion, as if he were trying to solve a puzzle and that puzzle were her. But *she* was not on trial, and she was not obliged to answer questions about herself.

"Yes."

"And if it *was* an accident—as you say it was—the fosterling would have had *ample* time to see you out walking and avoid shooting an arrow at you, wouldn't you say?"

Taliya felt herself flush with embarrassment. "I was skipping," she whispered.

"Pardon?"

"I wasn't walking. I was skipping at the time."

Craelyn blinked in surprise. From the Council bench, Erok snorted and Milahny cleared her throat discreetly. Taliya saw the humour in their eyes. Gods, they thought her a child! Taliya blinked back tears of embarrassment. *You are doing this for Bryndan*, she reminded herself sternly.

"-reflexes,"

"Lord Craelyn," King Allandrex warned.

Taliya took a deep breath. "Could you repeat that, please?"

"You must have remarkable reflexes to have ducked in time. How did you manage it?" Craelyn was staring at her intently.

Taliya twisted the ring on her finger. She saw the sorcerer's sharp eyes take in her ring, and she dropped her hands and tucked them behind her.

"Mother Jualis and Father Kilmar must be looking out for me," Taliya said.

"And Berech too, surely," Craelyn said.

Taliya shrugged, not wanting to agree with the sorcerer on anything.

"Thank you for your witness, Princess Taliya. You are dismissed from Council."

She curtsied and turned to walk away, taking her time. If anyone from the Council noted her dragging feet, they didn't comment on it.

"The Council has now heard from all witnesses," Lord Kade said. Taliya walked even slower, anxious to hear the outcome. "Lord Craelyn, after questioning Fosterling Bryndan, what is your recommended punishment for his crimes?"

"We have heard Fosterling Bryndan's truths, and I say that this crime calls for immediate and permanent banishment for Fosterling Bryndan—and all his family—from this court. Furthermore, his family's lands are to be seized immediately."

Taliya froze, then glanced over at Bryndan and grasped her resolve. She turned and strode back to the witness stand.

"Your witness is over, Princess Taliya. You no longer hold voice in Council," Lord Kade warned.

Taliya nodded acknowledgement, then curtsied to the Council. "I'm not speaking witness; I'm speaking for justice." A few Council members started whispering to one another, but Taliya ignored them and plowed forward. "My lords and ladies, I remind you that Bryndan is *our* fosterling. I don't care where his parents come from: they sent their son to us in good faith to raise as a loyal knight of Kilarya and he deserves the benefit of doubt for his actions. He is careless—and has *terrible* aim—but he is no assassin. Kilarya is a kingdom of truth and justice.

Bryndan has revealed his truths to the Council, but Lord Craelyn's recommendations are based on Bryndan's Gleniferite heritage, *not* Kilaryan justice."

Craelyn's eyes narrowed. "I am following Kilaryan law. I have determined-"

"You determined *nothing*. If he was truly guilty for attempting to kill me, he would already be in prison awaiting the gallows—his family with him. He is only guilty of misdemeanours."

Taliya glanced at the Council members. Whether or not she was officially permitted to speak, they couldn't stop themselves from hearing her words, and some of them, she noticed, were paying close attention.

"You overstep yourself, Princess Taliya. The Council does not recognize your voice at this time," Lord Kade warned.

She ignored him, her eyes returning to Craelyn. "Sorcerer Maddoux always follows Kilaryan law, and he always says that the greatest laws given to us were of *compassion*."

"Enough, Taliya." King Allandrex said in a tone of voice that instantly had Taliya closing her mouth.

She curtsied. "My apologies to the Council," she said as meekly as she could.

Allandrex was not appeased.

Erok raised his hand.

"The Council recognizes Lord Erok's voice," Kade said.

Erok looked thoughtful. "My lords and ladies, Princess Taliya *has* raised an interesting point. Sorcerer Maddoux has always been a voice of reason for us—and a voice of compassion. Berech's mouthpiece, if you will. But the sentence Lord Craelyn has recommended for Bryndan's *misdemeanours*," he raised an eyebrow at Taliya, "seems unduly harsh." Erok paused, then leaned towards the sorcerer. "No offense to you Lord Craelyn, but you are the youngest sorcerer in Kilarya's history and you have some large shoes to fill, and a lot of learning before you fill them."

Taliya's eyes widened at her cousin's brazenness. Erok—having just reached his major year—was a few months younger than Craelyn, yet he felt confident to lecture the sorcerer on his immaturity before Council. And yet, Erok *had* been on Council for the past five years, and Taliya knew that in that time he had gained the respect of many of the other Council members for his level-headed views.

Lord Kade approached each Council member and they spoke briefly, stopping last at the king's chair. He then returned to his place standing to the side of the Council chairs.

"The Council has heard all truths today and has come to a decision. Fosterling Bryndan, rise," Lord Kade commanded.

Talon and Jeo helped Bryndan to his feet, but he stood alone despite his shaking legs.

"The Council has heard witness, and has determined that the allegations of your attempted assassination are false. This incident is deemed an accident."

Bryndan put his hand to his mouth to stifle a sob.

"Your crime is that you shot an arrow in a forbidden ground which could have killed the crown princess. As you are a fosterling, your punishment shall be determined by Lord Jeo." Lord Kade looked at the training master, who had stepped forward. "I trust that Lord Jeo will find a punishment fitting for this crime that will satisfy the Council that this kind of incident will not happen again."

Lord Jeo bowed and Bryndan, after a short hesitation, followed suit. Taliya could see that her father's eyes were hard and unforgiving.

"Council is complete. Berech watch over us all," Lord Kade said.

Taliya turned to leave, sighing in relief that it was over.

Once outside the room, she caught Lord Craelyn's attention, and curtsied to him. "No offense was meant to you, Lord Craelyn. Sorcerer Maddoux's illness has been hard on all of us."

Lord Craelyn bowed in return. "I have much to learn, Princess, including humility. Berech knows that is the most difficult lesson of all."

He turned and walked away.

Taliya walked towards Sorcerer Maddoux's bedchambers, her legs heavy. She did not want this to be goodbye. She did not want to see the great Sorcerer Maddoux in such a state. She paused outside of his doors, sent up a silent prayer to Mother Jualis asking for his quick recovery to health, then knocked and pushed open the doors.

The sorcerer was being attended by three of the castle's shyliacs, but when they saw Taliya, they bowed and left.

"He is very confused," one of them whispered quietly on his way out the door. "We will be outside if he needs us."

Taliya stepped forward hesitantly, but when he moaned in pain she ran to his side and grabbed his hand.

"Oh, Sorcerer Maddoux." Taliya hated to see him looking so weak.

The old sorcerer opened his eyes and focused on her. "A mistake... was it a mistake?"

Taliya didn't know what he was talking about. She kissed him on his feverish forehead, as he had done to her so many times when she was growing up.

"No, Sorcerer Maddoux. It wasn't a mistake. You have done wonderfully."

"But the children... not all... not all the children were children! Not all... what have I done? Have I done well? ...Have I done right?"

Taliya's heart hammered in her chest. "What children, Sorcerer Maddoux?"

"You... they weren't... all... children." He gasped as if each breath hurt him. "All dying... we're dying... I didn't know... I didn't see until too late... And then what?"

He looked past her, and his eyes unfocused. "Watch them... keep them close..."

"Watch who, Sorcerer Maddoux? Keep who close?"

"He's delirious, Princess Taliya. Pay him no mind."

Taliya jumped at the sound of Lord Craelyn's voice. She turned and saw the young apprentice sorcerer leaning against the doorway, watching them. She didn't know how long he had been there.

"The Guardians! The Guardians!"

Taliya's heart began pounding in fear, and the hairs on the back of her neck stood up.

Lord Craelyn surged upright and strode forward.

"What Guardians, Master?" he asked urgently.

"I thought you said he was delirious." Taliya narrowed her eyes, but Lord Craelyn ignored her.

"Master, *what* Guardians?"

"The children! The children! Keep them close… watch them…" Sorcerer Maddoux shuddered and cried out. The three shyliacs entered the room, looking grim.

"Did I do right?" he asked one of the shyliacs. "Did I do right?"

Taliya moaned and stepped closer, clutching his hand to her chest. She couldn't leave him like this. He had always been there for her, always watched out for her. How could she leave him like this?

One of the shyliacs looked up from Sorcerer Maddoux. "Please leave," he said. Although the tone was polite, it was a command. Shyliacs held no titles or political sway, but they were the most powerful of healers and no one—not even the king himself—would disobey their orders when it came to a patient. Taliya kissed the kind sorcerer's hand and placed it gently down on the bed. She turned and dragged herself out into the corridor after Lord Craelyn.

The shyliac who had spoken to her turned back to his patient. He shushed the old sorcerer and stroked his head. Sorcerer Maddoux shuddered and closed his eyes, some of the lines in his face easing as he drifted into unconsciousness.

"Lord Craelyn, what does he mean?" Taliya whispered when she had shut the door behind her.

Lord Craelyn shook his head, not answering. He paced the hallway. Taliya twisted the ring on her finger, and the sorcerer's eyes focused on it.

Before she could stop him, Lord Craelyn had snatched her hand to examine her ring.

"Remarkable," he said, but his voice sounded hollow and far away. "Wherever did you get such a trinket?"

"I've had it since I was a baby," she said defensively.

"And it has fit you perfectly all this time?" His voice still had that hollow effect, as if his mind were far away.

She shrugged. "I suppose."

Craelyn twisted the ring around and stilled. Something in his face made Taliya tense.

"What do those marking say? It's foreign… definitely not Kilaryan."

Taliya snatched her hand back and clasped them behind her back, out of his reach. She twisted her ring protectively.

"I'm not sure," Taliya said brightly. "It might be meaningless."

"But it might not be. Allow me to have it investigated?"

Taliya brightened her smile, swallowing to hide her fear at the offer. "Oh, thank you. That's a very kind offer, but I'm fine. I'll let you know if I change my mind."

She took a step back and paused. "Lord Craelyn, what did he mean about the children?"

Craelyn closed his eyes and rubbed his neck for a moment. When he opened his eyes again, they focused on her. "Nothing, Princess Taliya. As I said, he was delirious."

Taliya stiffened her back so as not to flinch under the intensity of his gaze.

"But he wasn't. Not entirely. What aren't you telling me? Who are the 'Guardians?'"

The sorcerer gave her a half smile that didn't reach his eyes. Taliya took another step backwards.

The door was thrown open and the head shyliac marched out, looking grim. "The great Sorcerer Maddoux has passed into Berech's arms."

Taliya's hand flew to her mouth. Lord Craelyn's eyes widened.

The shyliac looked at Craelyn, and inclined his head in respect. "Sorcerer," he said. "I will inform Their Majesties at once." He bowed to Taliya, then strode down the corridor.

Craelyn rubbed his chin and looked tired.

Taliya stepped forward. She dipped a curtsy of respect, as protocol demanded.

"Sorcerer Craelyn," she said, fighting to keep her voice steady.

Craelyn bowed deeply in return, kissing her hand. "Your Royal Highness." He paused, staring at her ring until Taliya pulled her hand away. He had the same look as earlier; the one that made Taliya want to shrink away from him and hide.

She gave a brief nod, then turned to leave before her tears overflowed.

"Destroyers, Princess Taliya. They are destroyers."

"Pardon me?"

"You asked me who the Guardians were."

Taliya turned back to the sorcerer. "Destroyers of what? Children?"

"Of everything."

"What will you do about them?"

"Don't fear, Princess. I will search out any and all Guardians in this land, and if there are any to be found, I will destroy them first."

Taliya couldn't say why a shiver went down her spine. "For Kilarya's protection?"

"Yes," he answered. "For Kilarya's protection."

He bowed once more, then followed the shyliac's path down the corridor.

Taliya reached a hand back until she could feel the stone wall, then pressed her back against the cool, comforting surface. She closed her eyes and cried.

3

"May the mountains always shadow Glenifer of the west in protection, may the seas bless the Isles of Aminthia to the east with calm, may Kilarya of the south feel the winds of peace, and may the sun shine brightly on Imasdan of the north. That is our wish for our children, always." - From the religious texts of Eliva, as dictated to Andre the Prophet from Mother Jualis and Father Kilmar.

The knight drained his cup and tossed it on the ground.

"My, my. Aren't you the picture of knightliness," said a voice behind him.

"Shut up, Troy. Leave me alone."

Troy walked his way around to the front of Quand. His face was grim. "It's been over a month, Quand. Time to move on. Imasdan *needs* you."

The knight surged to his feet, and Troy took two steps back. "It will *never* be over. Not until I have the killer at the point of my sword."

Troy sighed and looked down at Quand's cup. "I know. But we've reached a dead end. Your squire wasn't the only one killed. Whoever it is picks people at random, it seems. The only commonality we've found is the black swan feather, which has been left with all the victims. The last victim—before your squire—was a young washer woman from a town near the Kilaryan border. She had never even been to Imald."

"You think I don't know that?" Quand snarled.

"I think," Troy said carefully, "that our king has kept you out of this investigation for good reason, Quand. You've not been yourself since your squire died. And the people are getting anxious. They need their hero back. The king expects-"

"The king has plenty of other knights to do his bidding. You, for one. Tell him I'm busy."

Troy's eyes flicked behind him, and immediately Quand knew his mistake.

"Oh, are you now?" The king asked mildly.

Quand closed his eyes, then turned around and knelt, fist on his heart.

"Forgive me, my liege. I meant no disrespect."

The king strode forward and put a hand on Quand's shoulder. After a moment, he dropped it again and his eyes turned hard.

"I have given you both time and space to mourn, Quand. But enough is enough. I have a task for you."

Quand bit his tongue and nodded. One did not refuse a direct order from the king.

"Stand, Quand." Quand rose from the floor. "I am sending you to Kilarya for a year. There are reports of civil unrest in Glenifer, and I need to get a sense of where Kilarya stands in this."

"A diplomatic mission, sir?"

The king shook his head. "A diplomatic mission would take months to organize and would require King Allandrex's written consent first. *But* a knight traveling alone is not bound by the same laws as our diplomats and can travel freely and without permission across borders. And you have reached legendary enough status in your ventures that even Kilarya has heard of you. They should be thrilled to have someone of your stature visiting them."

Quand shrugged off the compliment. "I have contacts in Kilarya, my liege. My old friend, Jeo, is a training master in the capital. I can write him and suggest I am interested in coming out for a year to visit. No doubt he'll ask me to help train his pages."

The king nodded. "I'll expect you to write him at once. You'll be leaving with the first warmth of spring."

"Is it so urgent, then?"

The king nodded. "It is."

"And what if it should come to war in Glenifer? Should I return?"

The king hesitated. "Not immediately. But keep on alert in case I call you back.

"Forgive me, sire, but if war is coming to Glenifer then I belong here, in Imasdan."

"You go where I need you, Quand. And I need you in Kilarya this spring."

Quand bowed his head in obeisance. "Of course, my liege."

"I expect you to send out weekly reports. In the usual manner, of course."

Quand nodded. He was well trained in the code that he would use for the reports—any reader who intercepted it would only see mundane chatter, but Quand would also be encoding information on Kilarya's army, political state, and any other important details his king should know.

"Even if it comes to war, the Gleniferites would be crazy to attack us. Our army is far greater than theirs."

The king flicked an annoyed glance at Troy, who bowed his head in apology for speaking out of turn.

"We may be able to defeat both Kilarya and Glenifer in a war, but I hope it doesn't come to that. Our people have lived in peace since my grandfather's day and by Father Kilmar I will *not* be the one to end that peace unless I must. Troy, you're dismissed."

The other knight bowed, fist over heart, and strode out of the room.

The king turned back to Quand. "There is another reason I need you there, Quand."

Quand nodded. Now it came to it. The king's speech about the diplomatic mission had been true, but he always had more than one reason for anything he did.

"I need you to travel there along the western border, near Glenifer. I know it will be risky and take longer, but I want to know what you see. How guarded is it; how easy is it to defend.

Glenifer would be mad to attack us, but Kilarya would be a tempting target for them. And in that case, Kilarya may request our aid."

"Then you intend to give it, my liege?"

The king shook his head. "I'm not sure yet. But I want to keep my options open. Also," he hesitated. "I want you to keep an eye on Sorcerer Craelyn and Princess Taliya."

"I thought it was Sorcerer Maddoux?"

The king shook his head. "I've heard news that he is dead. His apprentice is now the new sorcerer."

"What is it that I'm supposed to watch for?"

The king shrugged. "Nothing in particular. I know so little about him, and he is so new to his position. I need to know if he could ever be a threat to us."

"And Princess Taliya?"

"She is of marriageable age and is set to be the future ruler of Kilarya. I need to know what kind of ruler she is expected to be. I expect your weekly reports to be very detailed."

"Yes, my liege."

"Then I will leave you to your preparations."

Quand bowed as the king left the room, then sighed. He rubbed the back of his neck in frustration. He sent out a prayer for the gods to grant him mercy, for this year would show him none.

* * *

Not all the children are children. Taliya had spent months trying to figure out what Sorcerer Maddoux meant. She had broached the subject on multiple occasions with Sorcerer Craelyn, but he continued to deny that it was anything more than a dying man's ramblings. But there had been a tightness in his eyes and a tension in his shoulders that belied his words, and his eyes kept darting to her ring. Taliya had been growing more and more uneasy around him, and so she had stopped asking him about it altogether.

Instead, she had recruited her best friend, Juliette, to help her solve the mystery. The two of them had spent hours puzzling over it and reading through books about Kilarya's history to see if there was any mention of children not being children.

"I hear there are only four pages being named this year, Highness," Pallaster said, dragging Taliya's attention back to the present. "And *that* one—that Fosterling Bryndan—is one of them."

"And he hasn't attacked me with an arrow this whole winter!" Taliya said lightly. "I guess I was right all along about him."

One of Pallaster's maids covered her mouth and giggled, but quickly stopped when the red-haired one glared at her.

Pallaster snorted as she pinned Taliya's hair in place. "Shame, Highness! 'Twas a dreadful thing to happen to you last fall, and not to be made light of."

Pallaster paused and ran her hand along the black ribbon Taliya had ordered Pallaster to put in her hair.

"Are you sure, Highness? The time of mourning for our beloved Sorcerer Maddoux has long passed. Are you sure you want to still wear the black of remembrance? It might start upsetting the court."

Taliya turned to face the handmaid, effectively pulling the ribbon from Pallaster's grasp. "You mean it will upset Sorcerer Craelyn—that he will see it as a lack of honour to his new position."

Pallaster shrugged, her eyes respectfully on the floor.

The red-haired maid spoke up. "He is very young, Highness. He needs our support."

"He has it. Honouring Sorcerer Maddoux is not dishonouring Sorcerer Craelyn."

All three maids curtsied.

"Of course, your Highness. Forgive us for speaking out of turn," Pallaster said.

Taliya forced herself to relax. "You're dismissed," Taliya said, smiling to show she was not angry. They curtsied in unison and left the room with the door open.

Taliya's shoulders sagged when they left. They meant no harm. They couldn't know that the last few months the thought of Guardians attacking Kilarya haunted Taliya's dreams. She had combed through the library and even skirted the issue with Lord Kade, her uncle and history teacher. But Lord Kade knew nothing about the Guardians and couldn't understand what she had meant when she asked about the children.

Someone knocked on the door, and Taliya called for the person to enter.

"I'm to escort you to the Naming Ceremony, Highness," Page Allec said, bowing.

Taliya smiled at him and he nodded back, although he couldn't quite meet her eyes. They didn't know each other well, but what she did know about him she liked. She followed him, her stomach fluttering. Bryndan would be named.

After curtseying to her parents, Taliya slid into her seat beside her mother, schooling her facial expression into one of polite interest. Her heart jumped as the fosterlings entered. Taliya couldn't help but smile when she saw Bryndan at the front of the line.

The king was standing on the threshold.

"Fosterling Bryndan Gias," a knight commander called.

Bryndan stepped forward, beaming. He glanced at Taliya and a flush spread up from his neck. He coughed and bowed.

"Bryndan Gias," the king said as Bryndan straightened. "You came here four years ago at the age of 8 as a fosterling, to study and to learn. You now choose to remain here further, in the hopes that in eight years you might have earned the right to be called knight of this realm.

"Bryndan Gias, you've chosen to become a page of Kilarya. Who endorses this choice?"

A knight stepped forward. "On behalf of his father, Lord Gias, I endorse this choice."

"We ask you, Bryndan Gias, do you swear under Berech to follow the commands of all your instructors and all your superiors without fail and without question, that we might teach you what it means to be a page of Kilarya?"

Bryndan swallowed. "I swear."

The king lowered his sceptre to Bryndan, who touched his forehead to it, closing his eyes.

"Then we swear that we will protect you as our own and do all we can to ensure you become one of Kilarya's best. Bryndan Gias, we welcome you as a page of this realm."

Bryndan bowed once again before stepping back into place.

"Fosterling Yames Lu," the knight announced.

The next page had just stepped forward when Sorcerer Craelyn entered, his face grim.

He pushed the new pages out of his way in his haste to kneel before the throne. Taliya saw Bryndan stumble into another page.

"Your Majesties, I have received the most urgent of news." He dismissed the pages behind him with a flick of his hand. "The Naming Ceremony can wait. This cannot."

The king frowned and nodded to the guards, who herded the pages out of the room. Taliya found herself leaning forward. The Naming Ceremony had never in her lifetime been interrupted.

"What is it, Craelyn?" The king demanded.

"I've only just heard the news, majesties. Glenifer has been overthrown. The royal family is dead and the country is at war."

Taliya threw a hand over her mouth, but the king and queen remained motionless, though Taliya saw her father's arms tense as he gripped his throne.

"How much is rumour and how much is true?" King Allandrex demanded.

"My Lord," the queen's voice held a sharp warning. She rose from her chair.

The king turned and noticed Taliya.

"Taliya, my child, go and tell your cousins Milahny and Erok that they must attend me in the Council room. Then go straight to your classes."

Taliya flushed. "But I want to hear—"

"*Taliya*," the king chided.

Taliya clenched her fists. She rose and gave a stiff curtsy before stomping to the door.

"Gently, my dear," the queen called after her. "You aren't a herd of brawynns."

Taliya felt her back stiffen even more. She pretended she hadn't heard her mother, but she ceased stomping just the same.

As she left the throne room, one of the guards coughed into his hand. "'Twas bound to happen sooner or later," he muttered under his breath.

Taliya turned on her heel to stare at him, and he straightened, looking forward to avoid her eye contact.

"Mind your silence, sir," Taliya said, reminding him of his vows. The royal guards were all bound to silence with what they overheard in the courtroom.

The man blushed, and the other guard spoke up. "We keep the silence, Your Highness. Gord is newly promoted, but he will keep the silence."

Gord nodded and swallowed. "Apologies, Your Highness. I keep the silence."

Taliya nodded at him and turned away. As she rounded a corner, she caught a servant staring at her wide eyed. The young girl curtsied as Taliya went by, and Taliya sighed. If the servant had overheard anything it would be known throughout the whole castle by nightfall. Servants were not sworn to keep the silence.

Taliya went in search of her cousins.

4

> "So long as man has freedom to express himself, he will choose to disagree with his neighbour. Should that man be a king, and that man's neighbour be a king of a different land, then it is both our burden and our blessing to fight for that freedom." –From Yim Sandish, First Knight of Imasdan

"War!" Stascha hissed, leaning over to Taliya. "Can you believe it?"

Taliya shook her head. *Nightfall had been too generous*, she realized. It was barely after midday and already her friends were asking her about it. Lord Kade was apparently running late to teach their class, so Stascha was taking the opportunity to gossip.

"What's happened?" Juliette asked, thumping her books down beside Taliya.

Andreia stared at her wide-eyed. "Where have you been? Living in a drægon den? Haven't you heard the news?"

"I've been in the library, studying,"

"Is there an exam I forgot about?" Stascha asked, looking alarmed.

"No," Juliette said, with a reproving glance at Taliya. "I was wanting to know more about Kilarya's history."

Taliya mouthed an apology, and Juliette's shoulders relaxed. She and Juliette had planned to spend the morning after the Naming Ceremony doing some more research on Kilarya's history to see if they could find anything about children. But with Sorcerer Craelyn's news of the war, she had completely forgotten about her friend.

Stascha snorted. "Well aren't you a primrose?"

Juliette ignored the jab. "What news?"

"About Glenifer!" Stascha's eyes shone with the scandal. "My father's on the Council. He told me *everything*. They say the royal family has been killed. They say the palace has been invaded."

Juliette inhaled sharply. "That's awful!" She paused. "What will this mean for Kilarya?"

Everyone turned to look at Taliya, and she shrugged. "I don't know. We'll have to see what happens."

One of the other girls, Pash, sniffed quietly from her spot near the front and Taliya glanced at her. The girl's shoulders were tense and her eyes were red. She saw Taliya looking at her and her face tensed in annoyance. She rose and moved to a seat further away, refusing to look at Taliya and her friends. The message was clear: *I don't want your pity.*

"*Well*," Stascha said, tossing her hair over her shoulders, lowering her voice as she glanced at Pash and away. "If they had simply *fed* their people they wouldn't have had a rebellion."

"With what food, Stascha?" Andreia countered gently. "Glenifer has been battling storms and floods these last five years. I imagine there's hardly enough crops left to share around."

Stascha shrugged. "I don't know all the answers. Perhaps this is Berech punishing them." Yet despite her condemning words, she kept her voice down and her face turned from Pash.

Although she was one of her dormmates, Taliya did not count Pash as a friend. Pash was two years older than Taliya. She and her family had immigrated three years ago, and Pash spent her first year in the palace learning Kilaryan under private tutelage before she joined their classes. Pash's father was a second cousin to the royal family and a distant heir to the throne, although his interest had been more in research than in politics. He had been granted permission to visit Kilarya temporarily on the grounds of his research, which resulted in him uprooting his entire family and settling in Kilarya, with no mention of returning home. The Gleniferite king and queen had initially sent angry letters and delegates demanding their cousin's return, but as the crop shortages in Glenifer grew more and more, the king and queen focused on more internal affairs and left Pash's family alone. Pash's father was not, after all, high enough up in line for the throne to be a threat. Taliya wondered if this had changed overnight, with most of the royal family rumoured to have been killed.

When Pash first started attending classes with Taliya and her friends she took every opportunity to show Taliya how the Gleniferite way was superior, and had made a point especially of comparing Taliya to the Gleniferite royalty. At first Taliya had shrugged it off, but as time went on she found herself becoming resentful. She already had her perfect cousins, Milahny and Erok, showing her up—she didn't need the Gleniferite to also remind her of her flaws. And according to Pash, anything that wasn't Gleniferite was a flaw.

"Will we go to war?" Juliette asked Taliya.

Stascha's eyes widened. She had three older brothers that she worshiped, and all had taken vows of knighthood.

"I'm not sure." Taliya didn't like to spread rumours.

Lord Kade entered the room, his face grave. He glanced at Pash.

"Yes, well. I know you've all heard the grave circumstances our western neighbours are in. I'd like us all to spend a moment praying to Berech for their safety."

The girls kissed their fists before placing them on bowed foreheads while Lord Kade spoke a prayer. When he finished the blessing, he sighed.

"Of all the countries," he muttered to himself. "It has to be the one with the most renowned record keeping. I hope those sinners don't burn the books."

Lord Kade had spent years studying in Glenifer and frequently lamented the lack of written knowledge Kilarya had in comparison to its neighbour. Their teacher sighed to himself again. Taliya wondered ungraciously if he was more worried for the loss of lives in Glenifer or the loss of knowledge.

Lord Kade cleared his throat, "Yes, well. Let's continue on from yesterday's discussion."

A fosterling arrived before Lord Kade could say more, holding a note for the teacher. Lord Kade thanked the fosterling and sent him on his way. He scanned the note, his brow furrowed.

"Princess Taliya, the king and queen have requested your presence in their private chambers."

Taliya felt her heart leap, and it took all her self-control not to race from the room. She nodded gravely to Lord Kade and took her leave, her heart pounding.

Taliya arrived at her parents' rooms to discover that her cousins, Milahny and Erok, were already present and gathered around the table. She forced herself to smile at them.

It was evident from their postures and the notes scattered on the table that they had been discussing matters of state. While Erok was Taliya's elder by almost five years and Milahny a year older still, it hurt her that she had been invited late into the discussion. Her parents had promised Taliya that she would join Kilarya's Council at fifteen, just as her cousins had. Taliya reminded herself that Milahny wouldn't be impatient. Milahny would wait serenely to be invited to Council, and Taliya could too.

"You were speaking of Glenifer," Taliya said. It was a guess, but she managed to make it sound as if she knew the answer.

She curtsied to her parents when they looked up. Her father, Erok, and Milahny stood to greet her. Taliya's mother was not required by protocol to stand, but she smiled and nodded her head to Taliya.

Erok grinned and came to her. He kissed her cheek and ruffled her hair.

"Princess, your beauty is an extra light shining in this room."

Taliya couldn't quite hide her smile, but she gave her cousin a small shove. "Save your charm for your ladies, Erok."

He chuckled and escorted her to the table, offering her a seat as Milahny curtsied.

Taliya looked at Milahny's waist-long golden curls and Erok's own thick curls splayed across his forehead. She ran a hand through her own shortly cropped plain brown hair, feeling it turn greasier just looking at them.

Once they were all seated, the king continued the conversation as if he hadn't been interrupted. "We can't be sure. If he is, he'll likely head for Kilarya."

Taliya tried to keep up with the conversation.

"I disagree. He'll stay in Glenifer," Milahny argued. "He's 19 and—if anything like my brother—will be gathering up allies and seeking revenge, not refuge. It would feel like running away."

Erok nodded in agreement. Taliya twisted her ring as she thought over what she knew of Glenifer. The monarchs had two sons and two daughters. They must be speaking of Prince Damin, who was around nineteen. Taliya remembered that he was third in line.

The king shook his head. "The knights won't allow it. They'll want to keep him alive in case the royal line regains the throne. Their best chance of protecting him is in Kilarya. Mark my words: if he's still alive, he'll already be on his way here."

"Should we send an envoy for him?" Erok asked.

The king sighed. "I would if I knew for certain he was still alive. But Glenifer's army far surpasses ours, and I can't afford to stir up trouble if the line of succession is dead. Not until we have a stronger alliance."

Erok and Milahny glanced in unison at Taliya, then away. The king scowled down at the map he had on the table.

"We could consult with Lord Ollie," Taliya suggested, although it choked her to say it. Lord Ollie was Pash's father and—like his daughter—he made it clear his opinion of how Taliya stacked up when compared to the Gleniferite heirs. Not in so many *words* of course—a Gleniferite scholar would never abase himself to insulting someone in *words*. But a soft comment, accompanied with a sigh and a raised eyebrow of disdain could speak his message quite effectively.

The king sighed and shook his head. "Not yet. He is still a Gleniferite, and this might be his chance to make his bid for the throne."

"We are talking of the same Lord Ollie, are we not? The one who never leaves his rooms but sends servants to bring him books?" The queen asked with a small smile.

The king frowned. "He's not a concern right now. Let him keep doing what he's been doing these last few years. It's the prince that worries me, if he is even still alive. He is the wild card in all of this."

Taliya bit her lip and thought hard, desperate to prove that she belonged. She pointed to a spot on the map.

"If *I* were heading to Korign, I would cross here, at this river crossing. We could send knights out there to look for him."

Four heads turned towards her. Taliya swallowed hard but kept her chin up. She *would* contribute to their conversation. She *would* show them she had a right to be here with them.

Erok frowned. "That crossing hasn't been used in years. It's old and falling apart. I doubt there's even a workable ferry there anymore. The refugees have all been crossing further south, where the water is less turbulent."

"But that's the main road, where many of the villages are," Taliya disagreed. "Prince Damin and his knights would want the protection of secrecy until they arrived here. They don't know whom they can trust. He's still a squire, isn't he? His knight commander would insist-"

"His knight commander is the king, Taliya." Milahny said gently. "That's their custom."

"Well, the king would insist-"

"The king is dead," Allandrex said. "That is the one thing we know for certain."

Taliya flushed.

Allandrex rose. "My dear Taliya, it's late and we have asked you here for something else. We don't need to discuss this now." The king glanced at Erok and Milahny.

Taliya's two cousins rose as one, bowing their respects to Taliya and her parents before leaving the room. Neither of them looked at her.

Taliya blinked back stupid tears. She felt like she had failed a test.

The king paused and looked back at the map. His brow furrowed and he began muttering to himself, tracing lines in the air above the map. Taliya wasn't sure what he was doing.

Taliya fiddled with her ring nervously while she waited for him. "Not all the children are children." She mused to herself. She hadn't realized she'd spoken out loud until the king responded.

"Quite the prophet you're becoming, my dear."

"Excuse me?" Taliya's hands stilled.

"It sounds like some part of a prophecy." His attention was still focused on the maps.

Taliya's heart thundered in her ears. *A prophecy.* Not a page from Kilarya's history. A *prophecy.*

"Where did you hear that?" The queen asked.

"Sorcerer Maddoux said it. Before he died."

The queen inhaled sharply and the king straightened, giving her his full attention.

"Yes, well. Berech rest his soul, but I'm afraid Sorcerer Maddoux was no prophet," King Allandrex said sharply. "And he probably wasn't thinking clearly at the end. I wouldn't worry about it."

Then why are you worried about it? Taliya asked silently.

"That poor man." The queen sighed. "Berech give him peace. But Taliya, I see that you still wear the black ribbon to commemorate him. Time to move on, my darling, yes?"

She spoke it like a question, but Taliya knew it was a command. "Of course, Mother."

The queen reached out and took Taliya's hand. "Thank you, sweet. Taliya, my darling, we have a very important task you must undertake for us."

Taliya sat straighter, hope lifting her heart. "Of course. What is it?"

The king was avoiding eye contact—something he only did when he knew Taliya would be unhappy. "This is important, child," he said.

Taliya's stomach twisted. She pulled her hand from her mother's grasp and twisted the ring on her finger, a small piece of her still clinging to the hope that they were inviting her onto Council.

"Kilarya's facing uncertain times, child. With Glenifer in civil war, our western border is at risk. Refugees are coming in every day, but we can't allow the unrest in Glenifer to spread here."

It had to be about Kilarya's Council. It just *had* to be. Were they telling her she must wait a few more years before she would be invited onto it?

"Taliya, don't frown so, dear. It is unbecoming. Now, we've been discussing this problem with the Isles of Aminthia and they have promised us support should we need it," the queen said.

"But we need more than a promise," the king continued.

Taliya wondered if they had practised this speech before they had sent for her.

"And we need you safe—don't twist that ring, dear. A princess shouldn't fidget so."

Taliya's heart was hammering in her chest. She couldn't see where this was leading.

"You must go to Aminthia."

Taliya stared in horror at her father for a moment before his words sank in. She leapt to her feet. "But... but I can't!" she protested. "How can I be on the Council if I'm gone?"

Her parents looked confused. Taliya could have bitten off her tongue.

She tried another argument. "Surely travelling through the woods is too dangerous at this time. There are reports of- of robbers that hide in it. And it's practically still *winter*. No one travels so early in the year."

"Taliya," the queen sounded sad. She reached up and held Taliya's hands in sympathy. "We are not sending you to become a refugee. We are sending you to marry Prince Alastar."

Taliya's vision went dark and her breath caught in her throat. Should the prophet Elyan have shown up at that moment and announced the end of Eliva, Taliya would not have been surprised. She sank to the floor, tears in her eyes. "How could you?"

"It's for the best, Taliya." Queen Charlestte's voice broached no room for argument. "We'd planned to wait until your 16th birthday, but the unrest in Glenifer has forced our hand. We *need* this alliance with Aminthia. You must do this for us."

I won't go. The words were on Taliya's lips, but she couldn't speak them. Of course she would go; she had no choice. Taliya let her mother's words sink in. Political marriages were not arranged overnight. They had been planning this for a while. *On her 16th birthday*, they had said. That was less than a year away.

"Prince Alastar is the crown prince." Taliya twisted her ring, her heart hammering. *No. No, they wouldn't have... they* couldn't *have.*

The king started pacing and Taliya knew he was unhappy. The queen continued to hold Taliya's hands, stroking them with her thumbs.

"You never intended for me to be Queen of Kilarya. If I marry a crown prince, I'll fall under his kingdom." *Kilarya would go to Milahny.*

Taliya took a deep, shuddering breath and forced herself to think it through. *Kilarya would go to Milahny.* That would mean her parents were breaking the royal line. It would end with them and instead, go to the children of her father's younger brother.

"Why am I not to inherit the throne?" Taliya asked with numb lips.

There was no answer, and Taliya looked up at them and repeated her question. They exchanged a glance, and in it Taliya saw a world of secrets.

"What are you not telling me? What don't I know? Why can't I be Queen of Kilarya?"

There was another brief glance, a subtle shake of their heads. Taliya's heart grew cold. She was right about something. There was a reason she was not to inherit Kilarya.

Taliya clenched her fists. She wanted to cry, and scream. She wanted to shout at them, *what is wrong with* me? until they answered her, but she couldn't. Heiress she might not be, but she was still a princess.

"You're not telling me everything." Taliya said instead. Her voice came out strong and calm, but Taliya was numb inside. *No, not numb. Dead. I am dead.*

She understood now why they hadn't been training her to join the Council: they had never intended her to lead Kilarya. The crown would pass to perfect Milahny. Taliya did not know much about Alastar, other than the fact that he was crown prince of Aminthia and in his 22nd year. He had been fifth in line for the throne, until a plague had swept through Aminthia and killed half its population, including his four older sisters. Alastar had been studying in Imasdan at the time, but had returned home shortly thereafter to take his place as heir to the throne after his father, King Jastar. That had been a few years ago.

Her father stilled in his pacing and turned to her. "No, we're not," he admitted after a moment.

Taliya swallowed back her tears. "Tell me."

The king shook his head. "Hush, child. Of some matters, we cannot speak aloud."

"We've sent notice to King Jastar about the change in plans. We expect to hear his positive reply shortly, after which we'll make arrangements for your journey."

Taliya's head swam with the information.

The king took her hands and pulled her to her feet. He kissed her on her forehead.

"I'm sorry," Taliya whispered.

She wasn't sure exactly why she apologized. Perhaps it was because she felt embarrassed for crying, or perhaps it was because a part of her felt that if she had been a better person—more meek and obedient like Milahny—her whole world wouldn't be tearing apart.

"Don't apologize, daughter," the king said. For the first time since Taliya had entered their chamber, he looked her in the eye. "You've done nothing wrong. We know this is hard to understand and harder still to accept, but we trust you. You're strong, daughter, and adaptable. It may seem like we are sending you into the fire, but it's only because we know you'll come out the better from it."

"You're comparing me to pottery." Taliya offered a shaky smile, which her father returned. She saw her tears reflected in his eyes and wondered if her parents were feeling as shamed by their actions as she was.

"Life is a potter's wheel, child," he said. "The clay that cannot be shaped is useless. The pot that is too weak or too unbending cracks under pressure. It burns to walk through the fire-" Taliya thought of her nightmares about the fire and almost smiled. *She* knew that. "-but it will pass. Don't crack under the pressure, child. Come out of it stronger than before."

5

"The river Koris is a river teeming with life and bounty. It is because of Koris that I have chosen Korign to be the beloved capital of Kilarya. Within Koris' abundant arms, Korign will prosper." – From the Blessings of Berech

Bryndan stared at the map. "I agree. It *is* a crazy, stupid idea."

"But you'll come with me?" Princess Taliya asked.

He sighed. "We'll miss classes. Your parents will be frantic... they'll send out the army to look for you."

"Not at all! I'll have Juliette tell everyone I'm sick. The students will assume I've gone back to my royal rooms to rest, and Pallaster will assume I'm still in the student halls. It will be *perfect*. They won't even know I'm gone until after I've come back with Prince Damin."

"But what if you're waylaid? It's at least a day's journey to that river crossing, and you don't know how long you'll have to wait for them."

"It'll be *fine*, trust me. I'll leave a note for where they can find me if it comes to that."

Bryndan sighed and stared at the map again, tracing the route with his fingers.

"When were you thinking of leaving?"

"In two days, when we have a day off from classes. No one will question us heading out for a horseback ride in the morning and it will give us a head start."

"I could get in a lot of trouble for this," Bryndan said.

Taliya's eyes were glowing with excitement. Her jaw was set in a way that told him she had decided to go whether or not he was coming. *Of course* he was coming. He could picture the look on Lord Jeo's face when they escorted Prince Damin into the palace, everyone so grateful he had safely navigated the princess through the woods and brought two royals back safely. Taliya would give him a big kiss and tell everyone how brave he had been, how-

"I promise you won't get in trouble. I'll tell them it was my idea and I *dragged* you along. Please, Bryndan. I need you. I don't know the first thing about navigating through the woods."

"You'd be better asking a real knight," he grumbled, trying to hide the excitement pounding through his veins. They were actually going to do this.

"I *told* you. They'll just go speak to my parents about it, and my parents will stop us before we even get through the gate."

Bryndan chewed his lip, thoughtful. He was too pragmatic to believe he could be the hero all on his own. They would need help.

"I don't know enough about this sort of thing, yet. I'll need to ask someone else to join us."

Taliya looked deflated. "Who?"

"Allec. He's in his last year of pagehood and is really smart about navigation. He'll be able to look after us."

"Do you trust him?"

"As much as I trust you."

"Will he do it?"

Bryndan thought of how much Allec talked of adventure. With news of the civil war, Allec had requested to move to the borders and help with the incoming refugees. He had been devastated when Lord Jeo had flat out refused.

"He wouldn't miss it for anything. He'll be discreet, too. If you offer your protection to him as well, I know he'll jump at the chance. And he's *really good* in the woods."

Taliya nodded. "Then it's settled."

Bryndan nodded. "We'll be ready to go by first light, two days from now."

He watched her skip back into the palace and hoped he was doing the right thing.

*   *   *

Juliette caught her packing. She sat on Taliya's bed.

"Taking a trip?" She asked lightly.

Taliya nodded. "You'll cover for me, won't you, Jules? I should only be a few days."

Juliette gasped. "A few *days*. Taliya, *what* are you doing?"

"I can't say. Just trust me, won't you?"

Juliette folded her arms and a stubborn look came over her. "No. You've been acting weird since yesterday. I won't do anything for you unless you tell me what you're up to."

Taliya stopped folding her clothes and sat next to Juliette. She grabbed her friend's hand.

"You're sworn to secrecy about this."

Juliette looked insulted. "Since when do you not trust me?"

"Sorry, I know. I just…I've never done anything like this before."

"I know that smile, Taliya. You had that same smile when you told me you were going to raid the kitchen for cookies when we were younger. What's going on?"

"I'm going off to find Prince Damin!"

"The Gleniferite prince? You're going to *Glenifer*?! Are you insane?"

"No, no. Not to *Glenifer*. We think he's on his way to Korign, and I think I know which route he's taking. We're going to go find him and bring him back."

Taliya couldn't explain it. It wasn't about Prince Damin— not entirely. Gods willing, she would find and rescue Prince Damin, to prove herself to her family and the Council once and for all. Maybe if she did this, her parents would cancel her engagement and allow her to rule in Kilarya instead. With her *own* people.

"Who is 'we?'"

"Page Bryndan, Page Allec, and myself."

"Taliya, don't be stupid. You can't go off into the woods with those two."

"Why ever not?"

"It's *improper.* Your parents will throw a fit if they know you were alone with two boys. They're not exactly thrilled with how often you meet with Page Bryndan in the gardens, but at least there you're somewhat supervised with the servants and guards nearby."

"Oh." Taliya's face fell. "I hadn't thought of that. I guess I can ask Pallast-"

"Nonsense. Of course, I'm coming with you."

Juliette stood up decisively and moved to her dresser to pack her clothes.

"Oh, Jules, no. It's fine. Don't worry about it."

Juliette turned back to her, hands on hips. "Taliya, how could you even *think* of going on this adventure without me? I'm coming, or I'll go to your parents and tell them exactly what you're doing."

Taliya's mouth dropped open. "But you *promised.*"

"Oh, right. I did. Fine. Then take me with you, or I'll follow you anyway."

Taliya giggled at the mock stern expression on her friend's face. "You would, too."

Juliette nodded, her eyes sparkling with mischief. "To the heart of Glenifer, if it came to it." She placed one hand on her heart and the other hand on her forehead in a mock-swoon. "To the end of Eliva itself."

Taliya guffawed and threw a shirt at her friend, who ducked. "As if it would come to that."

A sad expression crossed Juliette's face, and her voice turned serious. "It could, Taliya. It really could."

Taliya opened her mouth to respond, but couldn't think of what to say. Before she could come up with something suitable, Juliette ran a hand through her hair and smiled. She picked up Taliya's shirt and held it above her head in triumph.

"To our next adventure!" she cried.

*   *   *

The guard waved them off at the gate. Four students going on a horseback ride on their day off was hardly anything to draw his attention, even if one of them had the hood pulled down over their face so he couldn't see who it was. Although it was warm for so early in spring, there was still a chill in the air and wearing a hood was not unusual.

When they were well into the woods, Taliya pulled her hood back around her shoulders. In the end, they had asked Andreia to cover for them. Andreia was a steady friend who was completely guileless. When Taliya had told her to tell others she and Juliette had feminine pains and were going to stay in bed, Andreia had merely nodded and said she hoped they would feel better soon. She had left a note tucked under her pillow in the student dorms saying where she was—if anyone—worried enough to look. Taliya wasn't sure what the boys had done, but neither seemed concerned about getting into trouble.

Allec and Taliya rode out front, with Bryndan and Juliette at a comfortable distance behind them.

Allec kept the pace brisk, but comfortable. When Taliya and Juliette reassured him that they were accustomed to long rides together and could manage the day with little breaks, Allec opted to eat lunch in the saddle and push on.

They passed a few other people on the road. Allec was on high alert and always gave Taliya a quick warning so she could pull her hood up. They wore their student robes to attract less attention from potential robbers, but Taliya didn't want anyone to accidentally recognize her face. To make it less obvious that she was trying to hide herself, Juliette also put her hood up when they passed strangers.

In between talk of their adventure and speculation over when they might encounter Prince Damin, Allec and Bryndan couldn't stop talking about Sir Quand W'len, the famous Imasdain knight who was travelling to Kilarya to train them.

"He's a *legend*," Bryndan crowed. "And *we* get to train under him."

"Is that usual, for knights to train pages from different realms?" Juliette asked. "It seems like a conflict of interest to me. What if we go to war against Imasdain?"

Taliya opened her mouth, but Allec jumped in before she could speak. "It's not usual, but it *can* happen. Well, obviously since we already know he's coming. He should be here within the next few days." He turned to Bryndan and the two of them began talking of all the different manoeuvres they wanted the legendary knight to teach them.

Juliette turned to Taliya and raised a questioning eyebrow. Taliya allowed the boys to ride ahead, while she and Juliette dropped back.

"He'll be here like a diplomat, but without all the envoys and permissions required."

"I wonder if he's handsome?" Juliette asked.

Taliya laughed. "Would it matter?" She teased her friend. Juliette blushed and glanced at Bryndan's back, then away. She had been stealing glances at Bryndan all morning.

"If we move quickly, we'll reach the river crossing by dark," Allec called back to them. "We can camp out there for the night and we can use the ferry to cross the river and scout the other side tomorrow."

Obligingly, Taliya and Juliette encouraged their horses to pick up the pace.

Although Taliya had reassured Allec she could handle the longer ride, she blew out a breath in relief when they could hear the river Koris ahead of them. Near the crossing there was a clearing that knights occasionally used to camp for the night. It had been unmarked on the map, but Allec knew where to go and led them there. After a brief discussion, they dismounted, and Taliya and Juliette led the horses to the river to drink while Bryndan and Allec started collecting wood to build a fire.

Taliya's muscles ached, but she bit her tongue and kept her complaints to herself. She had asked her friends to join her – it didn't seem right that she should whine about her discomfort. Holjack was not helping matters. He kept turning his head and trying to lead her off the trail into the forest. After the fifth attempt in less than an hour, Taliya lost her patience and swatted him on the neck.

"*Enough*, Holjack," she snapped. Holjack flattened his ears back but did not try to go off the trail again.

They had stopped at streams along the way, but the horses still drank with zeal and pawed the water. Once they were satiated, Juliette and Taliya brushed them down and tied them next to some grass to graze on. The girls then wandered back to the river to scout it.

Now that she saw it, Taliya began to doubt her judgement. Erok was probably right; nobody would cross here anymore. The water was frothing and churning and the rope for the ferry crossing looked old and worn.

Erok had mentioned there was a waterfall somewhere along this stretch, but Taliya couldn't remember if it was upriver or downriver from their crossing. But from the heavy rapids, it appeared they were well above the section where the river supposedly widened and smoothed out.

She scanned the far bank, but in the dimming light she couldn't see anything. No signs that Prince Damin was there. If he was even planning to cross through this area.

If he was even alive.

Taliya stared at the river, mesmerized by the water. She chewed on her lip. Her brilliant idea was becoming dumber now that they were actually here. Taliya didn't even know how to swim. Yet tomorrow they were planning to cross on the ferry and search the other side for signs of Prince Damin.

Juliette picked up some rocks and threw them into the river. "Take *that*, river! You don't scare us!"

Taliya snickered and picked up some more rocks. Giggling, the girls took turns throwing them as far as they could into the rushing water. Taliya barely made it halfway across but Juliette consistently got it close to the far shoreline.

Bryndan whistled appreciatively behind them.

"That's some throw!" he complimented Juliette.

To Taliya's amusement, Juliette—outgoing, flirtatious Juliette—blushed.

"You should see her aim!" Taliya teased. "Don't get on her bad side when she has a sling in her hand!"

Bryndan nodded seriously, but his eyes laughed. "Duly noted."

Bryndan glanced down at the ground, then picked up a rock and held it out to Juliette. "Look," he said, still staring at the ground. "This one's almost shaped like a heart. You should see how far you can throw this one."

Juliette took the rock from Bryndan, her face bright red. "That looks like a lucky rock," she said softly. "I don't think I could throw it."

Taliya glanced between them and then cleared her throat. "I'll go help Allec with supper. Why don't you, um… why don't you both go gather a bit more firewood before coming back?"

She turned and headed back to the campsite. As she was leaving, she heard Bryndan say, "If it's lucky, then it's yours."

Taliya laughed to herself as she left them alone.

Allec was whistling over the fire, appearing to be in good spirits. They had brought minimal food, not wanting to draw attention by carrying too much gear. Allec had brought food for two days. He had reassured Taliya that they could stretch it to three days and, after that, he and Bryndan could set traps and collect edible plants if it came to that point. Taliya knew they couldn't afford to stretch their stay longer than two days without setting off wide-spread panic in the castle, so she hoped that they would find Prince Damin before then.

6

All dræadons are dangerous, conniving creatures. They invade a man's mind in the most abhorrent of ways. In the name of Berech, they must be killed on sight." – Decree of Johnaston Allandrex Mikayle I, King of Kilarya in the year 429 of the First Age.

The next day they all examined the ferry. It was still floating, which was good. Allec tested the raft. He nodded in some areas and frowned in others.

"It should be fine for us. We can't take the horses unless we fortify it more, and that will take all day." He looked at Taliya.

Taliya looked at the river, her heart pounding. The waves seemed so much higher today than they had been yesterday, now that they were actually going to do this.

"We'll go ourselves and see what we can find. We don't have time to fortify it." She turned to Bryndan and Juliette. "I'll need Allec to help me cross, but *you* don't need to come."

Bryndan and Juliette glanced at each other and then turned back to her with scowls. "We're coming." Bryndan said stubbornly.

"It may take all of us to get this ferry across the river," Juliette added.

Allec nodded. "It would be nice to have some people on the riverbank just in case... but I think Juliette has a point. We might as well cross now. It will give us more time on the other side to see if we can find any signs of the prince."

They had opted to bring one saddle bag with food and a few essentials—just in case they couldn't make it back today. Bryndan tied it to the raft while Allec rechecked the balance.

Juliette grabbed Taliya's elbow. "You should tell them you can't swim," she whispered.

Taliya shook her head. "They'll just leave me behind," she whispered back. "It'll be fine. I'll just make sure I don't fall in."

Juliette glanced at the ferry and shivered. "Fair enough. I guess it wouldn't matter if you *could* swim. That water is freezing!"

Allec called them over and Juliette squeezed her hand before stepping onto the ferry.

"Right, Bryndan and I will need to stand to ferry this across, but I think we'll have better stability if the two of you knelt. Juliette, please come over here. Princ- er, Taliya, I'll have you right here, next to Juliette."

"Right," Allec said. "Now Bryndan, we just have to be careful to avoid that hole. See where that big rock is sticking out of the water, causing it to drop down around it? If we get caught in that we'll flip. But if we go there, and keep along this high line, we should be fine."

Taliya stared at the hole in question. It almost looked like a mini waterfall. She swallowed and twisted her ring around. She wanted to lay flat on the raft for more stability, but water was seeping through cracks in the bottom and she was loathe to get more wet than necessary. The water was frigid and her body already ached from cold—it was not a warm morning. The spray from the icy water added to her misery, but she bit her tongue. Nobody else was complaining.

Allec steered the raft with confidence and Taliya was grateful Bryndan had insisted he come along. Surely they wouldn't have made it that far without him.

Halfway across the river, the ferry wedged onto a partially submerged log and got stuck. Allec swore and pulled at the ropes, throwing his whole body into it, but the raft remained stuck, the wood creaking ominously. Taliya swallowed and crouched down lower. They were right above that hole Allec had warned them about.

"I'll help!" Juliette cried.

"No!" Allec shouted, but Juliette was already leaping to her feet.

The sudden movement caused the ferry to rock, and the current sucked the up-river edge, yanking it down into the water and pitching the ferry wildly to the side.

Allec threw himself backwards to pull the ferry back upright. The river released the up-current edge with a *pop* and the ferry shuddered. With a startled shriek, Juliette fell backwards into Taliya, knocking her into the water.

She popped up to see the other three still on the raft, Allec and Bryndan wrestling to keep it upright. Juliette was looking at her. At first Taliya thought she was smiling, but then saw her friend's face twist in horror and she opened her mouth to scream. Before she could see any more, Taliya was dragged over the rock and into the giant hole. Her nose filled with water and she coughed it out. Taliya fought the current hard, desperate for air.

Her lungs screamed and she panicked, thrashing in the water. The current pulled and dragged her in circles until she didn't know which way was up anymore. Her head cracked into a rock on the bottom, and Taliya opened her mouth to gasp, choking on water as it filled her lungs. Her body convulsed just as the river spat her back to the surface.

Taliya coughed and retched, trying to move her aching limbs to get her to the shore. She couldn't feel her hands or feet, and her limbs only moved sluggishly.

Get out before the waterfall, get out before the waterfall. She chanted to herself.

She kicked her legs hard, but the current relentlessly pulled her back under.

Get to the surface, get to the surface, get to-

*　　　*　　　*

Taliya coughed from the smoke, each breath feeling like her lungs were filling with tar. Her nose and eyes were both dripping and raging heat burned her skin. She stared across the room. The room was on fire and there was no safe crossing, but what she stared at was the other *Taliya.*

"*Taliya!*" Other Taliya cried, and in that one word Taliya heard despair—and a warning.

Neither Taliya was going to make it out alive. Together, *Taliya told herself—as she always did.* We should die together. *She began inching her way across the floor towards Other Taliya, and the slippers she was wearing began to burn her feet. Taliya stopped moving and started screaming in terror.*

"*Taliya!*" Other Taliya called out again, reaching out a hand towards her. *Light caught the edge of her eye and Taliya turned to it, then realized that she was the light; her hair was on fire. She threw her hands to her head in panic. She turned from Other Taliya and started to flee. But as she did so, blackness opened in front of her and Taliya felt as if two hands pulled her into it, leaving Other Taliya behind.*

"*Remember-*" the rest of what Other Taliya wanted to say was cut off by the blackness, and Taliya was left alone with her cowardice.

"*Elyan…*" The voice woke Taliya from her nightmare. She coughed and groaned, forcing her swollen eyes open. Her body was sore and for a moment Taliya couldn't remember why. She brushed her hand over her head to see if her hair was still there. It was. Slowly, the nightmare faded and memory returned to her.

"*Elyan…*" The whisper felt like a caress against her skin.

She had heard that name somewhere before. Was it her name? Or was she called something else? She couldn't remember. Her memories were filled with pain and cold. She closed her eyes.

"*Princess of the doomed…*" The voice called her attention back to the present.

Taliya couldn't see anyone, but someone must be close. All she could see was white. The silent voices continued to echo around her and it took effort to focus on what they said. She was so tired.

"*Eliva's Child…*"

No, she had heard it for certain that time. Yet nobody was there. She was all alone but for the sound of water. Taliya frowned. There was something about water… something that was important…

"Elyan Child…"

"Princess of the doomed…"

"Find the princess from the darkness…" The voices faded in and out together.

"Seek the friend from beyond…"

Taliya frowned. That was a line from one of Lord Kade's favourite prophecies. He recited it often enough to the class.

"The Other is coming…"

The hairs on the back of Taliya's neck stood on end, and she felt a cold fist press into her heart. Something in that voice—those words—broke through Taliya's fuzzy thoughts like a crystal shard to the heart. She gasped and forced herself to sit up.

The Other. Not a riddle, but a name. Taliya had heard that name before. Sometime long before she could remember. A woman's voice talking of *The Other*. A woman's voice that might otherwise bring comfort was cold with terror. It was a warning. But for what? Who was the Other? Taliya tried to speak, but could only cough, her body shuddering with the force. That last was definitely *not* part of the prophecy. That part was new.

"Come with us…"

"We will show you…"

An image burned in her mind of two worlds. One seemed to silhouette the other, as if they were both casting the exact same shadows onto the other.

What's that? Taliya had not the voice to ask aloud, yet the echoes answered her, ringing out at the same time. It took Taliya a moment to decipher them.

"Eliva's death…"

"Eliva's doom…"

"The shadow planet…"

"Eliva's end…"

Taliya had never liked riddles as a child. When Lord Maddoux used to give her riddles, Taliya would find a way to wheedle the answer from someone else. She shook her head, the effort sending sparks of pain through her skull.

"The Other is coming …"

"The Other is coming…"
"Soon, Elyan…"
"The Other is coming…"

Another image flashed before her. This one was of her ring. Taliya gripped the ring on her finger – it was still there. She twisted it, finding comfort in its presence.

"It is yours to give…"
"…but not his to take…"

"Who's to take?" Taliya croaked.

The voices spoke as one in a foreign tongue and her ring began to spark. Taliya wondered if they were reading the inscription on it – the inscription that no one could translate.

Between one breath and the next, the voices were gone. Taliya's vision cleared. She was lying on the bank, half submerged in the water. With effort, she dragged herself forward until her body was entirely out of the river. Her body was no longer cold and a part of her was concerned. Through the trees she could see the sun low on the horizon. Was it morning or evening? Her mind felt sluggish.

A part of Taliya wanted to lay still and sleep, but a niggling at the back of her mind kept her awake. She was forgetting something…

Taliya gasped, which turned into a spasming cough. *What had happened to her friends?* Had they made it safely back to the horses? Were they even now heading down the riverbanks, searching for her? Or had they gone home to alert the castle? Maybe they had split up. Maybe they had fallen into the river and drowned.

That last thought gave Taliya strength to force herself to her hands and knees. She was responsible for them; she had to be sure they were okay. She crawled up the bank towards the trees, her muscles protesting every movement. She couldn't feel her hands and feet. Her fingers were blue. Taliya stumbled forward, twisting her hand awkwardly as she did so. She straightened the limb and continued moving until she reached a tree. It took a long time.

Taliya used the tree to haul her aching body upright. She needed to find help. Korign shouldn't be far, but Taliya wasn't sure if she should head upriver or down. Growing up in the shelter of the castle taught her many of the shortcuts through the corridors, but navigating the woods seemed an impossible task.

But she had to keep moving.

The ring on her finger glimmered as it caught the sunlight. She had forgotten that she still had it… but then, she had never *not* had it.

The voices came back unbidden in her mind. *It is yours to give… But not his to take…*

Taliya pulled the ring off her finger with difficulty, running a hand over the strange writing. Taliya had known the ring protected her—it burned hot in warning when she was in danger, like when Bryndan had shot that arrow at her. But she had always thought that was the limit of its power. What further secrets did it hold? And what had they meant when they said, 'not his to take?'

An image of Sorcerer Craelyn holding her ring brushed through her thoughts, but she dismissed it. Sorcerer Craelyn served Kilarya. She tried to think of someone else that had shown an interest in her ring, but her thoughts were sluggish.

A breeze sent a shiver down her spine, reminding her of her situation. The ring didn't matter now; survival did. Her friends did.

She resolutely turned upriver, certain that if her friends were looking for her, she would find them. The water was still rough and fast, so she wasn't at the calm section of water yet. She might not have traveled far at all. Perhaps Allec was just around the bend.

She lurched along the bank, trying to be gentle with her deadened feet. Unable to keep her balance, Taliya stumbled from tree to tree. *Keep moving*, she chanted to herself, *keep moving*.

She hadn't been going for more than an hour when she heard something. Something that *called*. It was different from the voices that had whispered to her earlier. This felt more like something was reaching towards her mind, enticing her to follow it. Taliya turned and staggered a dozen steps towards it before she realized what she had done. She stopped, rubbing her aching head.

She glanced at the riverbank, then into the woods where the call had come from. Maybe it was her friends. Maybe she had heard them without realizing it.

I'll just go see if it's them. If it's not, I can come back to the river and keep heading upstream.

She turned into the woods, allowing her instincts to guide her. Every joint ached as if branded by a hot iron. She stumbled over roots and rocks and uneven terrain. Occasionally, she even stumbled over nothing as her legs simply gave out from under her. Each time she fell it became harder and harder to get back to her feet.

When the next root tripped her, Taliya lay down on her side and closed her eyes. Nothing was worth enduring another step. Not even life. She felt a buzz of magic kiss her skin. Taliya rolled onto her stomach and, cheek resting on the frosty forest floor, placed her hands palm down against the hard ground to better feel the magic. Her ring warmed in her hand—not a danger sign. It reminded Taliya of the palace cats when they purred and rubbed against her back home.

She felt a tug on her palms as the earth tickled her soul, and she surrendered to the magic, allowing its warmth to fill her. In her mind, Taliya saw two midnight blue eyes regarding her. They were beautiful and alien and they crinkled in amusement as they looked at her. Taliya trembled, but not with fear. *Drægon.*

The drægons were almost a myth in Kilarya. No one had seen a drægon for centuries; not since they had hidden themselves underground. Occasionally, a young man trying to prove his bravery would go in search of an entrance to their lair. Most returned with nothing, but some did not return at all. A few Kilaryans speculated that those who went missing had found their way into the drægon's lair only to be eaten. Pash— the Gleniferite—was one of the ones who insisted that the drægons were still hidden underground, biding their time before they returned to the surface. But most, like Lord Kade, said that was nonsense; drægons were extinct and the young men had simply died from other causes.

But they were wrong. The drægons weren't extinct; they were here. Taliya felt those eyes examining her, but she didn't feel like prey. Instead, she found herself oddly comforted by the drægon's presence in her mind, as if she had been waiting for it.

Her ring thrummed harder as that power brushed against her. Taliya felt the drægon eyeing the ring with interest and the power emanating from it intensified until Taliya felt as if her skin were crawling. Her breath caught in her throat.

It is yours to give…

Those alien blue eyes held her transfixed in their gaze. With shaking hands, she wiggled the ring off her finger and laid it on the ground beside her cheek, staring at it.

"Mine to give."

Taliya felt a scream rise up in her mind. Was it her voice or another? The vision of the girl in her nightmares—the Taliya who wasn't Taliya but who burned in the fire—came to her. She was still on fire, but this time she screamed at Taliya, that scream forming into words. *This is a mistake! You must never take it off! The ring bears power. It will only protect you as long as you wear it!*

The drægon eyes blinked for the first time. *We accept*, the drægon said in her mind.

In the next instant, the formidable presence of the drægon was gone—and so was her ring. Taliya searched for it, her numbed fingers feeling around in increasing panic. What had she done? *What had she done?*

A sharp emptiness cut into her at the ring's absence and Taliya let out a sob. She curled up into a ball, putting her hands across her stomach as if to protect her centre. But there was nothing to protect. Taliya felt empty inside.

7

"Blessed is he who stops for a stranger in the woods, for that stranger is truly a friend not yet met." – Kilaryan Proverb

Taliya opened her eyes to see a man grinning at her. She started and sat up, then clutched her head as it protested her movement. *A dream,* she prayed to herself. *Let this all be a terrible dream.*

"Why, I do believe we're sitting among royalty, lads."

She rolled to her hands and knees and vomited, and the man crouched next to her leapt back with a curse, as other men around her laughed.

When her vision cleared, Taliya looked around at the five men in the clearing, her heart thudding in her chest. Robbers. Robbers who recognized her.

She got to her feet slowly and the man who had spoken held out his hand to help her. He was older than the others and his beard was more grey than brown. Taliya slapped his hand away, and the other men jeered and hooted.

"Are you lost, Your Most Royal Highness?" Grey Beard asked her with a mock bow.

Taliya crossed her arms to hide their tremble and glared at the men. "I'm *fine.* I was separated from my party but they'll be along shortly. I suggest you leave before they find you."

Grey Beard turned and laughed at his men before turning back to her. He grabbed her by the upper arm and Taliya yelped as he yanked her close. His breath stank of ale and rot.

"Ain't nobody coming for you, Royal Highness. You're out here all alone. Whatever shall we do with you, heh?"

Taliya grabbed at his hand and tried to wrench it off her. His fingers dug in more tightly and his eyes narrowed.

"Naw, naw, Highness. There're lots of dangerous things in these here woods. You'd best stick with us. We'll see you get home safely and," his eyes skimmed down her body suggestively, "more or less in one piece."

"Less than more!" someone behind her jeered, resulting in more laughter.

Taliya kicked Grey Beard hard, right where Talon had taught her to do so. Grey Beard grunted and went down, but he did not release his grip and Taliya fell on top of him. She shrieked as another man grabbed her by the hair and yanked her backwards. She reached back and clawed the man's face and he swore. Another man— one who was missing a thumb— stepped forward and slapped her hard across the face, stunning her. Her hands were wrenched behind her back and her wrists bound tightly.

"Our little lost sparrow has some nasty claws," No Thumb said.

Taliya thought fast. *If my friends aren't here, they must have gone back to the castle. The knights will be out looking for me. They could even be close by.*

Taliya took a deep breath and screamed as loudly as she could. No Thumb covered his ears and snapped a kick that hit her in the stomach. Taliya flew to the ground, curling into a ball and heaving as her stomach spasmed.

No Thumb stepped over her and pulled out a knife. Taliya coughed, unable to draw breath as she rolled around on the ground in an effort to release the spasm, tears in her eyes.

Grey Beard came and stood next to No Thumb, his eyes cold. He waited until she was able to take a rattling breath and then grabbed the knife from No Thumb and put his boot on Taliya's shoulder, digging in until she sobbed.

"Go scout the area, make sure we're alone." He told the men. No Thumb stared down at her and grinned with cold eyes, while the other three melted into the woods.

"Now, we're reasonable men, Highness. But we're hungry men, too. The price the King will put on your head is enough to keep you alive." He took his boot off her and knelt down, grabbing her by the neck. "But it ain't enough to keep you whole, you understand? That stunt will cost you some of that pretty, little face."

He traced the knife along the side of her face and hot pain followed it. Taliya flinched away and he released her, standing up and wiping the blood off the knife.

"You do anything more and the price will be much higher. Maybe an eye or an ear. Or maybe-"

"Boss," No Thumb said quietly. "Ye hear that?"

Grey Beard stilled, looking around the woods. Taliya heard nothing except her heartbeat and ragged breath. She choked on her sobs and tried to take deep, calming breaths. Tried to ignore the throbbing pain on the left side of her face.

Grey Beard reached down and grabbed Taliya by the shoulder, yanking her to her feet. Blood dripped down her face as he pulled her tight against him, knife at her throat.

"We know you're there, cowards," Grey Beard called into the woods. "Face us like men."

"Alas, we have no girls to hide behind," a man's voice called from their left. He had a thick Gleniferite accent. Grey Beard whipped them around so Taliya was in between him and the man in the woods.

Grey Beard nodded to No Thumb, who drew another knife and stood with his back to them, watching.

"Refugees, heh? This here is no business of yours. Carry on, and I won't run you through."

"Oh, you could *try*," the man said. He'd somehow moved to be behind them, and again, Grey Beard turned them around to face the threat.

"Walk away." The Gleniferite said from the woods. "Leave the lady and walk away, and we'll let you live."

Grey Beard tightened his grip on Taliya, pressing the knife into her throat deep enough to nick her. Taliya whimpered.

"Nobody tells me what to do. *You* walk away, or watch as I slit her throat."

Behind them, No Thumb gargled. Grey Beard turned again and they watched as No Thumb grabbed at the arrow in his throat and collapsed to the ground.

Taliya cried out in terror, her chest heaving.

"Leave us alone," Grey Beard said, his voice catching in fear. He took a step backward, away from No Thumb.

"For the love of Berech, just-"

He pushed against her back, the hand holding the knife going slack. Taliya turned wildly to see him collapse, holding his sliced throat.

"I don't believe in Berech," the Gleniferite said coldly. He said something in his own language at the dead body, then wiped the blade clean and sheathed it. He crouched down with his hands open in front of him, watching her.

Taliya took a step back and hit something solid and warm. She stiffened, eyes wide.

"It's okay, it's okay. Easy now. I'm just going to cut these ropes off you," a man said from behind her.

Taliya shivered, but didn't struggle. The man behind her efficiently cut the ropes that held her wrists, and Taliya immediately stumbled away from him. Like the other man, he immediately sheathed his knife and held out both hands to her. He too crouched down, and Taliya saw that they were trying to calm her. It was working.

"We're here to help, lady. We're here to help," the man who had freed her said. He was older than his companion. He carried himself like a knight. Both had dark hair and tanned skin, more common to Gleniferites than Kilaryans, even if their accents hadn't already given them away. The beards on their faces looked at least a few days old, meaning they had been travelling in the forest for some time.

Taliya turned back to the man who had killed Grey Beard. He was young, just a few years older than her. His eyes were hard, but a twist to his mouth spoke of his pain and sorrow. Taliya took a deep, rattling breath.

"Thank you, Prince Damin," Taliya dropped into a shaky curtsy.

The prince stiffened, and Taliya knew she had guessed correctly.

"A prince fleeing his broken country," he said with bitterness, rising slowly to his feet. He bowed. "I'm afraid these are not the best circumstances for proper introductions, but I believe I know you as well, Princess Taliya."

Taliya did not feel like a princess at that minute. The slice on her face was still bleeding freely and ached something fierce, and the left side of her torn gown was covered in blood. She reached a hand up to touch her wound, but saw how dirty her hand was and dropped it down again. Damin's face hardened and his jaw clenched.

"We have some supplies to help clean that up, Princess," the man behind her said. She turned to him and he bowed. "I'm Tim. Please, let us help you clean that wound. It looks painful."

Taliya nodded and Damin held out his hand. Taliya hesitated, then accepted it, and he led her out of the clearing and back into the woods.

She glanced back at the two dead men and swallowed. "I… I guess the others are dead, too?"

"Two against five is not a good match. We had to even the odds."

Taliya shuddered at the coldness in his voice and Damin's eyebrows rose sarcastically.

"You would have preferred we left you to them?"

"No… I- no."

They fell into a silence as they continued walking. After a few minutes, they reached a small clearing near a creek and Taliya saw two horses tied to a tree, munching happily on some grass.

"How did you manage to cross the river with the horses?" She asked to change the subject.

"With great difficulty," Tim said, laughing. He pulled open one of the saddlebags and rifled around in it.

"If you don't mind, I'd like to build a fire and stay here for a bit. We'll need to disinfect that wound, and I think the heat will do you good." Tim eyed her.

Taliya hadn't noticed she was shivering until he mentioned it. Damin dropped her hand without ceremony. He grabbed a saddle blanket and held it out to her. The blanket smelled of horse and was crusted with dirt, but still Taliya hesitated.

"I'll get blood on it," she warned.

Damin cracked a small smile—the first one she had seen on him, although it didn't reach his eyes. "Don't worry. I won't lose sleep over it."

Taliya wrapped it around herself gratefully, sinking to the ground. Damin nodded in satisfaction and set off to gather firewood.

The two were efficient, and held the comfortable silence of a pair who had done this enough times that they didn't need to speak as they each set to their tasks. In almost no time a pot of water was boiling over the fire. Damin removed the pot to let it cool then dipped a clean cloth into it. Taliya dreaded what was to come next.

To distract her, Tim launched into a story.

"These are some fair woods you have here, Princess Taliya. Reminds me of the days when I went hunting with my ole knight master. If you could have seen the man! As large as a bear and as quick as a rabbit, he was. I remember a time when we stood facing two score of outlaws—*two score!*—and us surrounded. I was shaking in my boots, but not ole Staro, no. He told them they could lay down their weapons and surrender nice and pretty, like." Tim roared with laughter at the memory and launched into another tale of the indomitable Lord Staro.

Damin's hands were gentle, but it *hurt*. More than a few times she flinched away from him. Always he stopped and waited until she calmed before he approached her again.

"Are these stories true?" she asked Damin quietly.

Damin shrugged. "I've heard them a dozen times over this journey and they've varied little. But I know Tim's folks were bards."

When he had finished cleaning up the blood, Damin wiped the area with a salve. It stung a little, but mostly it was cooling on her skin. Finally, he bandaged it up and sat back.

"I'm so sorry, Taliya, but I'm afraid it's going to leave a scar."

Taliya shrugged, but her eyes filled with tears. "That's all right," she lied.

Damin looked unhappy with her answer. She wanted to tell him it wasn't *his* fault, but her throat tightened, and she couldn't get the words out. Damin looked away from her and glanced up towards the sky. It was already getting dark.

"I'm sure your parents are worried sick for you, but it's late in the day and I don't like the horses to walk in the dark. Are you okay if we camp here tonight?"

She glanced around the woods, pulling the blanket closer. "Are we safe here?"

"As safe as anywhere. The bandits are all dead," Damin said.

Taliya hugged the blanket closer. "They didn't have to die," she whispered.

Damin frowned. "Yes, they did."

"You could have just tied them up and left them."

"No, I couldn't have. That would have been crueller."

"Would it?"

Damin poked at the fire with a stick. Tim put another pot of water on to cook some food, unusually quiet after all his stories from earlier.

"Taliya, you don't understand these things."

Taliya hated hearing that. She heard it enough from her family at home, but to hear it from a refugee barely a few years older than her was too much.

"Explain it to me then," she snapped.

Tim cleared his throat and muttered something about chopping more wood before it got dark.

Damin poked at the fire for another minute before running a hand through his hair. He pulled out a black swan feather, and began to toy with it. "Okay, okay. It's like this. We are two men against five. If we had left them tied up they would have found a way to escape and come after us, at which point *they* would have had the advantage. They would have killed Tim and I and recaptured you—which would not have been a pleasant ending. And even if we managed to tie them up and bring them back to your kingdom for justice what then? The damage they had done to you was a death warrant. And most men would prefer a quick, clean death by the knife than the noose.

"And let's say we *had* let them walk away, and they *hadn't* come back and killed us. Still, all the knights of the kingdom would have been sent to find them, because the king and queen could *not* let them get away with what they did to you without starting an uprising of protest. And in that case, the knights would have looked for the quickest solution to the problem. So if they couldn't find the men, they might pick some innocents to put to death instead. Believe me, Taliya. I've seen this all before. The minute they laid hands on you they had signed their own death warrants. Tim and I just made sure it was a swift and merciful death."

Taliya stared at the fire. "It was still *wrong*."

But was it? It didn't *feel* so wrong to her. She was relieved they were dead. Did that make her a bad person? Those men might have had families and loved ones who would miss them. They had said they were hungry... maybe they were desperate. Taliya fingered the bandage on her face and glanced at Damin, who was glaring at the fire. Damin, a refugee prince fleeing from his own country who had still stopped to help her when he heard her scream. *Desperate men can still have honour,* she thought.

Tim returned with more firewood. He paused when he saw Damin playing with the swan feather and frowned.

Taliya gestured to the feather. "Is that from your family?" she asked gently.

Damin looked down at the feather in surprise, as if he hadn't realized he was holding it.

"No," he said, carefully putting it away. "It's from the man who murdered my family. He left one with every royal member he murdered—including me, only I escaped."

"Jualis, I'm sorry," Taliya said. She paused. "Does the feather mean anything?"

Damin didn't say anything, so after a minute, Tim said quietly, "A few years ago, people started getting killed. The killer marked the kills with a black swan feather. We don't know what it means. We didn't even know—before now—that the victims receive the feather *before* they are killed."

Taliya didn't know what to say, and so she sat with them in silence. She didn't feel much like eating, but Taliya knew she needed her strength, so she forced the food down slowly.

After dinner, they pulled out some bedding and laid it down for Taliya.

"What about you?"

Damin shrugged. "We've had worse nights than this. We'll be fine."

The ground was cold and hard despite the bedding, so Taliya didn't protest any more. She wrapped herself gratefully in their blankets, careful to lay on her right side.

"Taliya?" Damin asked after a moment.

She yawned. "Yes?"

"This may be rude, but what *were* you doing out here on your own?"

Taliya flushed, glad her face was hidden in the shadows.

"I was looking for you," she said.

"On your own?" Damin sounded horrified.

"Of course not. My friends came with me, but... we got separated on the river." Taliya thought back to the raft and her swim down the river. She giggled at the hilarity of her day. Not long after, the giggles turned to tears and she began crying quietly.

She jumped when a hand lay on top of her head. She hadn't heard Damin approach.

"Shh, it's okay. I'm sure your friends are fine. You'll be home tomorrow, and no further harm will come to you."

Taliya wanted to tell him that it was foolish to make such promises, but his words were comforting and his hand stroking her head felt warm and strong. She cried until she had no more tears.

8

"The truest knight is not sung of by the bards, for he is a knight who serves humbly unto his death and works not for his own glory. Seek not to please the fickle nature of people, but to please the everlasting justice of the Gods." – From Yim Sandish, First Knight of Imasdan

Quand had travelled without rest for the past two days and even his bones ached with weariness. He was in no hurry to reach Korign, but he dared not stop along the way. The roads had become unsafe to travel, even for a knight. His travels near the Gleniferite border had been grim. The flow of refugees was endless, and while the Kilaryans were opening their homes in compassion, Quand could see that all those extra mouths would be a burden come next winter, unless more support came from Korign.

His horse pricked its ears and the knight stopped. He had not been deaf to the birds startling nearby; someone was close. He drew his sword. These woods were not kind, and he had dissuaded more than a handful of bandits from attacking him on his journey. Quand sat still in the saddle, waiting patiently for the group to approach from the woods. They sounded too loud to be bandits, but it didn't hurt to be cautious.

"Oh!" The gasp came from a maiden.

She was, perhaps, the only one of the raggedy group who was surprised. The knight appraised the three strangers.

The first thing he saw was the maiden's bloody dress and the bandage on the side of her face. She looked weary, swaying slightly as she sat on the horse. A young man led the horse with one hand, a short sword in his other. An older man sat mounted on a second horse, his sword also drawn and lying discreetly across his lap. The two men were Gleniferites, likely refugees. Quand hadn't seen many refugees on this road, but their torn and stained clothing gave them away. They held their swords with a confidence that declared they were knights. The three men stood at silent impasse.

"Grace of the Gods, Sir knight," the maiden said in greeting. Her voice sounded strained as she spoke in his language, and Quand could hear the Kilaryan accent.

"Grace of the Gods, travellers," the knight replied in Kilaryan, sheathing his sword.

After a few breaths, the two Gleniferites followed suit, although the man on the ground appeared reluctant to do so. He took a protective step closer to the maiden, his young eyes assessing.

"What brings a knight of the northern realm to Korign?" the maiden asked after it became apparent no one else would speak.

The knight gave a small bow from his horse, but kept a sharp eye on the two Gleniferites.

"I am here under invitation from the Kilaryan training master, Lord Jeo," he said. "I am to serve this next year in Kilarya, under King Allandrex."

"Then you must be Sir Quand W'len of Imasdan."

She bowed her head in greeting. "I am Princess Taliya, of Kilarya. I present to you my companions-"

"Darryl and Tim," the young man jumped in. "We're refugees from Glenifer. We came across Princess Taliya in distress and offered our services."

The princess looked surprised. She opened her mouth to say something, then glanced between Quand and the young man and shut it again.

Of course he would meet the princess on the road. One of the two people his king had told him to watch. Quand almost rolled his eyes. Mother Jualis must have a strong sense of humour today. And he hadn't missed the interruption of the young man. They were lying, then. Heavens help him; Quand was a simple knight and he liked it when things stayed simple. Meeting the princess and her two lying companions on the road did not a simple life make.

He bit back a sigh and dismounted to kneel before the princess. Whatever their story, he had little choice but to hold his peace and accompany them to Korign. To do otherwise would dishonour his realm.

"On my honour, Princess, I'm delighted to make your acquaintance and am sorry for the trouble you had. Allow me to accompany you home, since Korign is also my destination." Sir Quand paused before he remounted his horse. "You seem a bit fatigued," he hedged. It was an understatement. She looked as if she were about to fall from the saddle in weariness. "By your leave, you may ride my war horse with me. That way, your friend *Darryl* may ride the mare you're on. It would speed up our journey."

The princess hesitated and bit her lip, glancing at Darryl.

Darryl scowled, but gave a curt nod and helped Taliya down from the saddle. Between Quand and Darryl, they helped her onto his horse and the young man vaulted onto the mare's back.

At first, Taliya held herself away in the saddle. Then the older man, Tim, jumped into a story about his former knight commander, a Lord Staro, as if he had been interrupted earlier. As the tale went on Taliya began giggling at some of the more ridiculous deeds of this knight and settled into Quand. Darryl rode closely beside them. He did not glance in their direction, but Quand could feel his attention.

Not more than an hour into their journey, a vision of midnight blue eyes burned into Quand's head. He tensed and gripped his sword, looking to the skies. The tree canopy was thick, and he couldn't see clearly. The vision grew stronger.

"Hold!" he called.

"What's wrong?" the princess asked.

"Brawynns," Quand grunted.

Sweat beaded on his forehead as the vision grew stronger. He leapt from the saddle before the vision crippled him, then unsheathed his dagger. Quand sliced his palm with his dagger and placed it on the ground. Jualis knew the reason, but making a blood offering to the earth was the only way to clear the pain from his head.

He could see Darryl and Tim doing the same thing.

"What are you doing?" Taliya sounded frightened.

"A blood sacrifice to Eliva works. I don't know why, but it works."

"What do you mean?"

"Have you ever seen a brawynn attack, princess?" Darryl asked.

She shook her head. "There are no brawynns in Kilarya. We drove them out before I was born."

"We get them all the time in Imasdan," Quand said grimly. "Before every one, I see a set of eyes in my mind—midnight blue drægon eyes." He heard the princess gasp, but he was too focused on the skies to look at her.

"I see them, too," Darryl said quietly. "It starts after you see your first brawynn. And after that, the image grows stronger every time. And more painful. It can drive a man crazy if he doesn't offer a blood sacrifice to Eliva."

"That stops the vision?" Taliya asked with a strange note to her voice.

Quand shook his head. "No, but it takes away the pain that comes with it and makes it tolerable. We need to find an area we can make a stand, if it comes to that."

"There, to the left. We can use that tree to guard our backs." Darryl pointed, and the group made its way to the tree, the three knights dismounted with the princess still in the saddle. The tree Darryl led them to was so large, its trunk dwarfed them and all their horses. It was a good place to face the brawynns, who would attack from the sky. The three knights remounted their horses and drew their swords. The horses shifted on their feet and blew out of their noses nervously.

"I can see it too, those eyes," Taliya said quietly. "But it doesn't hurt me."

Quand stared at her. "You've seen brawynns before?"

She shook her head. "I told you, we don't have them in Kilarya." She shivered. "At least, we didn't before now."

Quand frowned. "Then how can you see the blue eyes?"

She shrugged. "I just can," she said in a small voice. She rubbed her hands together, staring at them.

Quand didn't have time to puzzle over it. Maybe it was because she was Kilaryan.

"The drægons are their masters. The more exposure to brawynns you have, the more their master crawls inside your head," he warned her. "It can drive a man mad."

Darryl frowned at him, then gave a warning glance at Taliya. Quand saw her shiver out of the corner of his eye. "It is not so bad as that," Darryl said. "I've never thought of it as a bad thing, to have warning that the brawynns are near. But it is good to be careful with such unpredictable beasts."

"Will they leave us alone?" Taliya asked in a small voice.

Quand shrugged. "In Imasdan they attack us when they can, and we return the favour. Glenifer, it appears, has a more amiable relationship with the beasts."

"Not what I'd call 'amiable,'" Tim grumbled. "More like a wary ceasefire."

"They bring no wind with them," Quand murmured. "They only bring the wind if they are on the attack. We may be safe, for now."

Taliya sucked in her breath. "*There*. I see them."

Quand focused up as three brawynns circled above them.

From a distance, one could be forgiven for mistaking it for a winged horse. But instead of hooves, its back feet ended in talons that could grip a branch, and its front feet looked like a lion's paws with large retractable claws. One could always tell if a brawynn was attacking by seeing if their claws were out or retracted. These ones, Quand could see, had their claws retracted. It didn't mean they were safe, though.

They dropped down below the canopy and perched on tree branches. When one of the branches creaked ominously, the brawynn switched and used its front legs to grip into the side of the tree. All three of them opened their mouths to grin at them, revealing two rows of razor-sharp teeth—good for ripping and tearing into their prey.

"We are travelers," Quand shouted up at them in Kilaryan. He wasn't sure if they understood the language, but he didn't want to tell them that he was from Imasdan, in case that was enough to make them attack. "But you will find that we are not easy prey. Find your food elsewhere, beasts, and leave us alone."

They didn't respond but continued gazing at the travelers, twitching their tails and gnashing their teeth together. One by one, all their gazes focused on the princess.

"She is ours, and not for a snack," Darryl growled in Gleniferite.

The brawynns looked at Darryl and hissed what almost sounded like a laugh, then looked back at the princess. The stench of their breath crossed the distance and Quand felt bile rise in his throat. The horses, distant cousins to the brawynns, were wary but not frightened. The brawynns didn't attack horses, and Quand had seen for himself that the beasts were loathe to go after anyone on horseback. He wasn't sure what these ones were doing. They seemed curious, more than anything. Curious about the princess.

Quand couldn't see her face, as she was mounted in front of him, but he could see she was watching them, and her shoulders were stiff.

After another moment, the beasts took to the skies once more. A few minutes later and the drægon eyes faded from Quand's mind.

The group let out a breath.

"What was *that* about?" Tim asked, glancing at Taliya. "They sure were interested in *you*."

Taliya shrugged helplessly. "I have no idea. Why would they even *be* here? Why would they have come back to our country?"

Quand sheathed his sword. "Unpredictable beasts," he muttered. "Who knows why a brawynn does anything? Perhaps they're hungry. Or perhaps they're looking to expand their territory back into Kilarya once more."

Taliya frowned. "I'll have to tell my father about them."

"With the brawynns appearing this close to Korign, I'm sure he already knows," Darryl said. "We should keep going. They left us alone this time, but I don't like being so exposed in these woods. There are too many dangers here."

Taliya rubbed her arms but said nothing in response as they continued on their way.

It was not more than a few hours when some of the search party found them. Or rather, a group of pages and their arms teacher.

"Grace of the Gods, sir knight. What- *Princess?*"

"Bryndan!" Taliya cried. "You're all right!"

She swung down to the ground gracelessly. She might have fallen had Quand not caught her shoulder in time. She ran forward and the boy caught her up in a hug.

"*I'm* all right?" The page's voice was muffled. "We've been worried *sick*, Taliya! Praise Berech you're alive."

Beside him was another man whom Quand recognized. Jeo, the training master approached with sword drawn and face grim.

"You need a shyliac," Lord Jeo told Taliya without taking his eyes off the knights.

Taliya shook her head. "I'm okay. Dam- eh, they helped me." Taliya waved to the Gleniferites, then swept her hand wider to indicate Quand as well.

"Bryndan, escort the princess back to the castle. Yames, run ahead and warn them she's coming. Tell them also that she is accompanied by three foreign knights." Jeo said.

His eyes flashed in recognition at Quand, but they remained hard and cold. The pages snapped to attention and turned to the knights, holding their training staves at the ready. Quand's respect for Jeo increased tenfold. The youths would not stand a chance against three trained knights, but they were attending to Jeo's subtle command that he and the Gleniferites were potential enemies. The princess and Page Bryndan made their way steadily to the castle gates, the page's arms around the princess to help support her.

"You may wish to dismount and identify yourselves before the guards arrive," Lord Jeo said.

Quand nodded and did as requested. "Lord Jeo, you remember me. I'm Sir Quand W'len of Imasdan. I'm here at the request of my king to work alongside you for the next year."

Jeo nodded, but did not offer any more in the way of formal greeting. He wouldn't—not until they had been questioned and cleared of guilt.

Darryl and Tim had also dismounted, but when Jeo looked at him Darryl raised his chin. "I'll speak to King Allandrex."

Quand looked up to the heavens in frustration. Only a Gleniferite would be so arrogant as to demand an audience with the king when they were under suspicion of harming the princess. Jeo was treating them civilly, but Quand knew not to trust that polite tone of voice.

Jeo stared for a long moment at Darryl and the pages shifted from foot to foot, their hands fidgeting over their weapons. Tim stepped closer to Darryl in silent support. Jeo glanced at Quand, who shrugged. He would not take responsibility for the insult the young Gleniferite gave. They had been drawn together for a similar purpose, but any alliance had ended when Princess Taliya had left them.

"Your request is witnessed, *sir*," Jeo snapped.

Quand let out a breath of relief when more soldiers appeared.

One of the other soldiers stepped forward. "I'm Talon, Captain of the Guards. You will kindly disarm and follow me to the castle. My men will look after your weapons and horses until such a time as they may be returned to you."

Quand complied, taking pains to keep his movements relaxed and slow. The captain was within his rights to bind them as prisoners, but he was allowing them to enter the castle as free men. Quand had no desire to show resistance. He had nothing to hide and to imply otherwise would be unwise. The knight glanced at the Gleniferites, but they were also obeying orders. Perhaps they too realized that entering the castle unbound would be the only dignity granted to them.

Quand rubbed his neck. He hoped that this start was not a sign of what the next year in Kilarya would bring.

9

"Who is Elyan? Is he come to destroy Eliva or save it? I believe it is neither of these. Elyan is merely a witness. He is not come to interfere, but to mark the passing of this world." - From the Elyan Prophecies

Bryndan dragged his feet into the stables to complete his rostered duties. He would give up a full year of his life if it allowed him to spend that afternoon in the castle. All anyone could talk about was Princess Taliya's safe return and the knights who accompanied her—and one of them was *Prince Damin*—the very person for whom they had been searching. The other pages were still inside, but when Bryndan lingered with them Lord Jeo had sharply reminded him of his duties in the stable. His precise words had been, "You've had enough fun gallivanting around, Bryndan. Your punishment has still not been determined, and I suggest you keep your head down until it is." Allec had been sent to the kitchen to scrub pots.

After they had lost Taliya, Allec and Bryndan had manoeuvred them back to the shore. Allec wanted to go looking for Taliya, but Juliette shot that idea down.

"We could spend days looking for her, and we don't have supplies. We need to get back to the castle and raise the alarm. The knights have better resources to search than we do."

Reluctantly, Bryndan and Allec had agreed, so they had thrown saddles on the horses and taken off as quickly as possible. For almost two days, Bryndan had been desperate with worry. Jeo had forbidden the pages to help in the search and instead forced them to continue their training as if the world wasn't crashing down around them. But then she came back, and she was all right. Bryndan thought about her bloodstained gown and the bandage on the side of her face and amended, *mostly all right*.

Trelk was lounging on a bale of hay as Bryndan approached. The small boy hesitated. Bryndan had assumed Trelk would be at the castle with the rest of the pages. He suppressed a shiver when Trelk caught sight of him. The large boy leapt to his feet and stalked towards Bryndan like a cat on the hunt.

"My horse's tack needs cleaning," Trelk snarled, towering over Bryndan.

Bryndan kept his eyes down and tried to step around the taller boy.

"Did you hear me, brawynn dung?"

Bryndan felt his temper surfacing. Another time, he might have offered to clean it since he was on stable duty anyway. But he was grumpy that he was not inside the castle with his friends hearing all the gossip.

"I heard you," Bryndan snapped, taking a step back. He glanced in vain for the stable master. Perhaps the stable master was at the castle, too. Where Trelk should be, and where Bryndan wished he were.

"And?"

"And what?"

Trelk's eyes bulged out in shock at Bryndan's defiance. "You're going to clean it, is what."

"Clean it yourself," Bryndan snarled.

Trelk stepped closer until Bryndan's nose almost brushed the boy's chest. Bryndan tipped his head back to glare at the large boy.

"You are lower than scum, brawynn dung. Your whole family should be wiped off the surface of Eliva. You aren't worthy to lick my boots, but I'll even let you clean my horse's tack."

Bryndan flushed. "Let it go, Trelk. It wasn't my fault."

Trelk's hand tensed into a fist. "You should watch who you pick a fight with, brawynn dung."

"Shame, boys, shame," Jeo snapped.

Relief surged through Bryndan. He turned and bowed to the training master, praising Berech that their instructor had arrived. Lord Jeo's face did not have its usual sardonic expression. Instead there was a thunder in his eyes that had Bryndan swallowing. He had never seen the training master so angry.

"Our princess has just returned safely and you're here squabbling like roosters. What knights will you be if you care more for your bickering than your rulers? Both of you shame me. Trelk, you're not on stable duty. Why are you here?"

Trelk said nothing.

Lord Jeo's eyes narrowed. "Give me your sword."

Bryndan carried no training sword—he wouldn't until the Choosing Ceremony in summer—but he flinched all the same. *Surely* Jeo was not asking Trelk to give up his training sword... such a punishment had never been done. Trelk's hand flew to his hilt and, for a second, Bryndan worried he might challenge Lord Jeo. After a tense moment, Trelk unbuckled his belt and passed the sword to the training master.

"I don't want to see you near these grounds for the next month. Not to watch, not to train. Do you understand?"

Trelk nodded once, his lips pressed together so tightly they were white.

"You'll report to Lord Kade, the history teacher, for that time. You'll take on any extra assignment and perform any duty he asks of you. I'll explain this to him tonight. Do you understand?"

Again, Trelk nodded.

"Get out of my sight."

Trelk obeyed, his back stiff as he stalked out of the stables.

Lord Jeo turned his piercing gaze on Bryndan. The small boy shrunk down a little more.

"Bryndan, next month you will go in the arena against Trelk."

Bryndan flinched. "But *sir-*"

"You're afraid of him, boy. You carry the sins of others and let him walk all over you for it. Stand up for yourself a little more. That tragedy was none of your doing."

Bryndan winced.

"I can't allow this to continue. Bryndan, you've always been a doormat for Trelk. No knight of mine will be a doormat for anybody. Either you can handle being a knight or you can't. You're not far behind on the skills, but whenever you spar with Trelk you just give up. I've seen you. Defend, defend, defend, but never any *attack*. You're disappointing me, Bryndan. I've given you a month to decide what you want for your life. Take some initiative for once and stop letting Trelk bully you to the ground."

"But, sir, I *do* take initiative. I accompanied the princess-"

Jeo held up his hand. "*Don't* remind me of that. The Council still hasn't met to determine your punishment, and they will be calling on *me* to make a recommendation as to a suitable punishment for you and Allec. If you're lucky, I may just leave you and Allec on stable and kitchen duties until the summer festival. But if you keep trying my patience I'm sure I'll think of something less desirable."

Bryndan flinched and bowed his head.

Lord Jeo sighed. "I'm not being cruel, Bryndan. But I don't think you fully understand what you did. If the princess had been killed, you could have faced the same fate. Disobeying rules to go gallivanting around in the woods is stupidity."

Lord Jeo glanced down at Trelk's sword. "I'm not expecting you to *win* against Trelk, but I expect to see *something* that will convince me you still belong here. You'll face Trelk in the arena, or you'll be sent home."

It would be humiliating. Bryndan was the fourth and youngest son. His eldest brother stayed home to run the estate he was to inherit. Bryndan's second oldest brother was a knight and currently on tour near the Imasdain border, while Thom, who was just a year older than Bryndan, had fallen off a horse two years ago and could no longer walk. If Bryndan failed out of knighthood, his father would be shamed.

"Have you ever seen a sparrow in the forest, Page Bryndan?"

Bryndan's brow furrowed at the change of topic, but he nodded.

Lord Jeo continued, "You compare it to a hawk and you would think that for such a little bird to take on a foe ten times its size is suicide. But that little bird has pluck, Bryndan. When a courageous sparrow goes against a large hawk, I wouldn't always bet my money on the hawk."

Jeo stepped forward until he was within an arm's reach of Bryndan. "I'm trying to find that sparrow in you, Bryndan. Berech knows it's been hard. Show me that you have what it takes to be a knight of this realm."

"The sparrow also knows when to hide from its enemies," Bryndan offered, his eyes on his feet.

He glanced up to see the corner of Lord Jeo's mouth tightened in disappointment. He turned and walked away.

"You'll fight Trelk, or you'll pack your bags," he ordered over his shoulder.

Bryndan clenched his fists as he watched the training master sent away.

"That one," said a man from behind him, "has the look of murder in his eyes."

"Jeo?" Bryndan asked, turning around. He was surprised to see Prince Damin and Tim behind him.

"Trelk," Damin corrected.

Bryndan shrugged. He didn't want to talk about it, especially with the Gleniferites. "What are you doing here?" he asked instead.

Damin showed his teeth in what might have been a smile. He sat on the edge of a hay bale. "Horses are far better company than people sometimes. And besides, I'm nosy about this new court I find myself in, and sometimes the best gossip comes from the lessers."

Bryndan did not like being referred to as a 'lesser'. He crossed his arms.

"Oh, so you're a spy," he snapped.

Damin laughed. "Just curious, little page. Just curious. I notice things. For example, I notice that when Trelk looks at you, it's not an 'I don't like you' look. That's an 'I'll kill you when I get the chance' look."

Bryndan looked away. "It's not your business."

"True enough, little page." Damin rose from the hay bale and nodded to him.

Tim approached and put his hand on Bryndan's shoulder.

"As my ole knight master used to say, 'obsessing over the sins of others is like drinking poison because you want them to suffer.'"

Bryndan looked up at him. "What does that mean?"

"It means you'll have burdens enough in your life without adding the burdens of others to your heart." He smiled kindly, then followed Damin outside.

10

"I have given my blessings to the rightful rulers of this land, and righteous they will remain down to the very last descendant. When I return, it will be to kiss the brows of their children's children's children and say unto them, 'well done.'" – from the Prophecies of Berech

"Thank you. Yes, you've done an amazing job. See? I'm all better now. I just needed to rest." Taliya spoke in a gentle voice to the agitated shyliacs, who fretted over her bedside. She had been asleep for two days, they told her. Otherwise, Taliya had not been able to gather much useful information from them— so concerned were they with fluttering around her.

Taliya was in her royal rooms instead of the student halls. She had cried when she awoke and realized her parents weren't by her side. But she wasn't sure whether it was from disappointment or relief. What would she say to them? Were they avoiding her out of anger, or were they simply too busy with other royal duties to attend their daughter?

Taliya sighed. She wished that—just once—her parents would put her above their political duties. Her hands clenched under the sheets and she willed herself to be calm.

The shyliacs talked amongst themselves and Taliya wished they would just leave. She reached for her ring before remembering that it was gone. She rubbed her hands together instead, feeling empty inside.

"Princess!"

Taliya looked up at the welcome voice. Pallaster ran to her side and knelt on the floor by the bed, clutching Taliya's arm.

"Oh, Princess, Princess!"

The shyliacs tried to shoo the handmaid away and Taliya found that she had reached her limit of tolerance. She looked at the head shyliac.

"Leave me, please." Her voice was firm. "All of you. I appreciate your help, but I need you to go."

"You're unwell, Princess."

"I was, but now I'm not. *Please leave.*"

The head shyliac bowed in consent, his face impassive. The others followed his lead and retreated out of the room.

Taliya turned back to Pallaster, stroking the handmaid's bowed head with her free hand. "Oh, Pallaster. I'm so glad to see you."

Pallaster reached out and touched the side of Taliya's face. The shyliacs had nodded in satisfaction over Damin's work, then put more pastes and salves on it. But Damin had been right; it was going to leave a scar. Right now, that scar was red and angry, but the shyliacs promised that within a few months it would start to fade.

Pallaster's eyes teared up as she looked at the scar. Taliya forced herself to smile.

"It's nothing. Doesn't even hurt anymore and the shyliacs say the redness will fade shortly."

"You're still beautiful."

Taliya's own eyes teared at the kind words. It shouldn't matter to her how Pallaster said she looked. It *shouldn't.*

"Pallaster, will you help me?"

Pallaster swallowed and withdrew her hand, then stood up and brushed off her skirt, all business.

"I need to find my parents. And I need to find out what happened to the knights who helped me." Taliya couldn't believe she had forgotten them.

"Of course, Princess." She smoothed back her hair, then proceeded to help Taliya dress.

"May I say, Princess, you truly know how to pick handsome rescuers. And a *prince*, too," Pallaster added cheekily.

So the truth of Damin's title had made its way around the castle. Taliya wasn't surprised. Pallaster was as efficient as ever as she helped Taliya change into a proper gown.

The handmaiden hesitated, then pulled out the black ribbon to weave into Taliya's hair. Taliya gripped her hand to stop her. So much had happened in the woods – so much had changed.

"Not today, Pallaster," Taliya told her. "I can honour Sorcerer Maddoux without wearing the black. I think it's time I move forward."

Pallaster bit her lip and nodded, gently placing the black ribbon back ribbon down. She selected a different one.

"This one, perhaps?" She suggested. "To honour the Gleniferites who saved your life?"

It was red and gold – Gleniferite's official colours. It was perfect. Taliya nodded, and Pallaster expertly weaved it through her hair.

When the handmaiden was done, Taliya asked the guard outside her door where her parents were.

"The Council chambers," he grunted.

Taliya faltered a step. It still hurt, knowing that she would never sit on Kilarya's Council.

"They did not want to leave your side, Princess." Pallaster's voice was small and uncertain. "They left this morning to speak with the Council."

Taliya didn't turn to look back at her faithful handmaid. Pallaster knew how Taliya felt about her parents. She might be making this up, to ease the princess's sore spirits.

*　　　*　　　*

Taliya was surprised to find Damin and Tim present alongside her parents, Milahny, and Erok. None of them looked pleased.

Taliya gave a small smile to Damin as she curtsied. Pallaster was right; he *did* look well. He had shaved off his beard and wore clean clothes, as did Tim. Damin's eyes skimmed over her as if he didn't really see her, and Taliya's smile faltered.

She glanced over at Milahny; Kilarya's new crown princess. Did Milahny know it yet? Or worse, had she always known that she was to be the true heiress to the crown? That Taliya—for whatever reason—didn't have a proper stake in the claim? Taliya shook the thoughts from her head. She didn't have time for that now. She turned her focus to her parents, who had risen and were striding towards her.

"I'm glad you're safe." Her mother reached out to hug her.

"Me too," Taliya agreed, returning her mother's hug.

"We have had a terrible few days, Taliya," her father said. "What in *Berech's name* caused you to pull such a stunt? And to involve your friends as well? For shame, Taliya."

Taliya pulled out of her mother's embrace. "I-"

"The woods are *dangerous*, Taliya. You were almost killed! If Prince Damin hadn't heard you screaming and come to your rescue you might have wished you were dead."

Taliya took a deep breath. "Don't punish them."

Allandrex paused in his pacing. "Excuse me?"

Taliya took a step forward, heart pounding. "My friends. Don't punish them for what happened. It was my fault they were there. I dragged them into it and threatened to go without them. They only wanted to help me."

"Taliya, what you all did cannot go unpunished," Milahny said gently.

"But you're all young. Any punishment should reflect your youth and inexperience with the world," Erok added, glancing at the king.

Taliya almost snapped at him that he was barely a few years older than her, but she held her tongue, since he seemed to be on her side.

Allandrex reached forward and gently touched Taliya's scar, then took her hands in his. "I think you've been punished enough, Taliya. I don't think you'll do something like that again."

Taliya shook her head fervently.

"Besides, you found who you were looking for," Erok added with a twinkle in his eye. "And you were right about where to find him, in the end."

Taliya flushed. She had forgotten Damin was here. She couldn't bring herself to look at him. Instead, she kept her gaze on her father.

"Please, father," she said quietly. "*Please* don't be too hard on my friends. They would never have done this on their own."

Allandrex sighed. "I will be fair."

It was the best she could do for them, so Taliya nodded her agreement.

"If you'll excuse us now, Taliya. We were about to have a Council with Prince Damin and Sir Tim to discuss Glenifer's situation."

"*King* Damin, sir," Damin corrected.

Allandrex frowned. "You have not been crowned yet, lad."

Damin flushed. Tim put a hand on his shoulder and Damin clenched his jaw and nodded curtly.

"Taliya-"

"No," she interrupted her father.

He raised his eyebrows at her. Taliya swallowed and reached for her ring before dropping her hands again.

"You were about to dismiss me, but I will *not* be dismissed. These men saved my life, my lord. I owe them a debt. I'd like to stay and hear what they have to say."

The king gave a small smile. Taliya imagined that Tim looked surprised, but Damin's scowl remained.

"As you wish." He gestured for her to be seated at the table. "But when we're finished, you will see Sorcerer Craelyn. He is waiting to see you, now that you are better. He wants to find out more about those robbers in the woods."

Taliya suppressed an involuntary shudder at the memory.

Allandrex turned to the prince. "We cannot send my people into your country, Highness. Kilarya has always maintained a policy of non-interference into the internal affairs of others."

"My lord, Raspin is a cunning and devious traitor. He killed my entire family." Damin took a breath before continuing. "Nothing good can come if he remains in command. He's power-hungry, and he won't stop the slaughter at Glenifer's borders. Raspin wants to control all of Eliva. Kilarya would be next in his sights."

"What my lord prince says is true, lord king," Tim agreed. "Raspin is Prince Damin's bastard brother." He glanced in apology at Damin. "He was raised in the palace, but he doesn't have a claim to the throne. It'll be a disaster, Your Majesties. The refugees you've seen entering your country up to this point are a trickle compared to the flood that will come. We can stop this madness, but we need Kilarya's support."

"I won't send my people into someone else's war." King Allandrex was resolute. "Your words may be true. But for now, I'll continue sending in spies to gather information on what is happening. If Kilarya goes to war against Glenifer, it will be because I see no other option. This is not a time for rash actions."

"Sir, he is claiming himself Elyan, the prophet returned," Damin said.

Allandrex went very still. He exchanged glances with the queen, but neither spoke.

"Is he mad? False prophets are burned." Erok was horrified.

Taliya sucked in her breath. "They burn false prophets?"

At the same time Damin said, "He killed my whole family and claimed the crown for his own. I think it is safe to say he is more than a little mad."

Erok glanced at Taliya and answered her question. "Everyone does, Taliya. Berech decreed it."

"*Father Kilmar* decreed the burnings. We don't believe in Berech," Damin jumped in.

Erok shrugged. "It's useless to argue religion." The phrase, *especially when you're wrong* went unspoken.

"And we're getting off point," Milahny reminded everyone.

Taliya glanced at her parents, who were being oddly silent during this exchange. She saw the queen give a slight shake of her head and King Allandrex stood up, signalling the end of the meeting. The others stood up as well. Damin did so last, looking frustrated.

"I don't think we'll reach a conclusion today. The queen and I have other matters to attend. Damin, we will think on what you have said, but we will not act without sound cause or reason." The king hesitated, then put a hand on Damin's shoulders.

Quietly, he said, "You must know that at full strength we could not win a war against Glenifer without the aid of allies. We hope to build strong alliances soon," his eyes darted to Taliya and away, but not before Damin caught the look, "but we need time to decide what is the best course of action for Kilarya."

The king took the queen's hand and they began to make their leave from the Council chamber. Taliya bit her lip. She wanted to speak up to defend Damin, but would her father listen? Perhaps if she had been on Kilarya's Council she would understand more... Taliya clenched her fists. Wishing for the impossible was a waste of time.

"Father? What about the brawynns?" Taliya asked.

The king frowned. "I've heard all the reports coming in. They started making their way across the border at the same time as the refugees. They've been terrifying the smaller towns near the border but have not attacked any of the villages or the farms yet. I don't like that they're here, but we don't have enough resources to deal with them right now. Not with all the unrest in Glenifer."

"So, they'll stay?"

"For now. I have sent out orders that no one is to provoke the beasts. I'm hoping that we can maintain the same alliance that the Gleniferites did with them."

Damin snorted. "Not so much of an alliance, King Allandrex."

The king shrugged. "Regardless, we cannot defend ourselves against both the brawynns *and* the Gleniferites—if it comes to that. And so, if the brawynns hold their peace with us, we will extend them the same courtesy. For now."

Taliya nodded. They didn't have a lot of other options. She prayed to Mother Jualis that the brawynns continued to leave them alone. After seeing the beasts, she wouldn't want to send anyone to stand against them. Gods help them if the brawynns ever decided to attack. Her father was right, their country had enough problems to deal with already.

"Taliya." There was a warning in the king's voice. "Sorcerer Craelyn is waiting."

Taliya glanced at her father's face and decided that she would not try her luck defying him again. She dragged her feet to the corridor. She couldn't help glancing back at Damin, but he was deep in whispered conversation with Tim and did not acknowledge her.

The queen leaned over to her. "We'll be having an official presentation tomorrow night, to honour the knights who rescued you," she murmured. "Are you well enough to present the gifts? It would put our people at ease to see you performing your duties."

She glanced at Taliya's scar and pressed her lips together, but didn't say anything. Taliya nodded and her parents glided away. It was a long time after they left before she worked up the courage to go to Sorcerer Craelyn's chambers. She didn't want to talk to him about what had happened. It was humiliating and… personal. And how could she ever explain about the voices? If they burned false prophets at the stake, what would Sorcerer Craelyn say if she told him about the voices? She swallowed as she approached the sorcerer's rooms. She reached up to knock on the door and saw her bare finger, the imprint of the ring still evident. She hesitated. Had she made the right decision in giving it to the drægons?

Taliya tapped her knuckles once on the door and withdrew her hand quickly. Perhaps he wasn't in. She should come back later. She'd already taken two steps down the corridor when the door swung open. Craelyn smiled down at her, sweeping a deep bow.

"Your Highness, what a relief to see you back here where you belong."

"Thank you, Sorcerer Craelyn." Taliya struggled to form the words as he escorted her into his chamber. His *interrogation* chamber. Taliya's heart pounded and she broke into a cold sweat. *He is* not *my enemy*, she reminded herself firmly. *He doesn't have to be—not if you keep the part about the voices to yourself!* And what if she did tell him that part of the story? At best, he would think she was crazy. At worst, he might call for her to be burned at the stake. She shuddered. Death by fire already haunted her nightmares; she couldn't handle the thought of facing it.

There were two chairs set up, and two cups filled with cordial sat waiting. He escorted her to a chair and offered her one of the cups, then picked up his own drink and tilted it to her in salute.

"To your safe return."

Taliya took a cautious sip and the fluid helped moisten her dry mouth. The silence became awkward. Taliya took another sip. She meant to appear confident, but she was shaking so much that the cordial spilled onto her hand. Craelyn offered her a handkerchief and Taliya mopped her hand, flushing. She handed the wet handkerchief back to him, not looking at his face.

"I know this is difficult, Princess Taliya, but I'd like to hear your story from the beginning."

"From when we left the castle?"

Craelyn waved a hand dismissively. "No, no. I heard a lot of it from your friends. Why don't you start with how you pulled yourself out of the river and end with meeting the pages in the field?"

Taliya talked. She told him everything that had happened—barring the voices, of course. She didn't mention her missing ring, and glossed over the time after she met Damin and Tim. Still, by the end of her retelling her voice was sore, and she had drained her cup dry. Craelyn refilled it with more cordial and Taliya answered all his questions as best she could.

"And I see you lost your ring, too. Or did you take it off?"

Taliya reached out to twist the ring on her finger, then stopped mid-gesture. "I don't know where it is," she said, which was partly the truth. "I must have lost it somewhere. Maybe in the river?"

"Of course. What a shame. I'm sure the king and queen would be delighted to request a new one be made for you."

"Of course," Taliya agreed politely.

He sat there in silence, waiting for something, as if he knew she hadn't told him the full story. Taliya decided to turn the tables on him.

"And how about you, Sorcerer Craelyn?"

"I beg your pardon, Princess?"

"Have you found them?"

"Found who?"

"The Guardians. Have you found them yet?"

Caught off guard by her question, Craelyn surged to his feet. Taliya suppressed a smile at his reaction.

"No, and it *bothers* me. Guardians are aggressive. I should have seen a sign of them by now. It worries me that they might be hiding among us, waiting for something."

"What would they be waiting for?"

Craelyn threw his hands out in exasperation, pacing the room. "I don't know."

"Would it have something to do with the children?"

He paused in his pacing with his back to her, and Taliya saw his shoulders tighten a fraction before they relaxed. He turned around. He had a slightly condescending smile on his face, but Taliya believed the tension she had seen more than his words.

"You are still fretting about what Sorcerer Maddoux said? I've told you this before Princess: he was confused and sick. He didn't know what he was talking about."

"But you believed him about the Guardians."

"The Guardians are enough to have *anyone* worried, whether he spoke truly of them or not."

"Then what about when he spoke of the children not being children?"

"I don't recall him saying any such thing."

"Yes, you do," Taliya insisted. "You're lying to me."

The sorcerer's face darkened. "Be careful whom you accuse of lying, Princess. We, all of us, have our secrets, don't we?"

He glanced at her empty ring finger and Taliya quickly hid her hands in the folds of her skirts. It was as if he *knew* what she had done with her ring. But how could he know? Taliya's thoughts were in turmoil, and her throat closed off in fear. How much of her story did he know was untrue? She glanced back up at his face, but his eyes were hooded and she couldn't read his expression.

They stared at each other in a stand-off. Finally, Taliya rose to her feet and the sorcerer bowed his head to her.

"I'm sorry, Princess. But I don't answer to you."

"I'm the crown princess. You answer to the crown." Taliya had meant to sound assertive, but her tone was whiny even to her own ears. She flinched inwardly but stiffened her shoulders and raised her chin.

Craelyn shook his head. "I'm sorry, Princess. But you're not the crown princess anymore. I know about your betrothal—and what it means. And even if you were, there are only two people on Eliva whom I answer two. One is the king."

"And the second?"

"Berech, of course. I acknowledge no higher authority than our great prophet, Berech. Only He can judge me for what I know, and for what I do.

"I believe I've tired you enough for the day, Princess Taliya, and I thank you for letting me hear your *truths*." There was a subtle emphasis on the last word. He punctuated her dismissal with a small bow; not the bow that a sorcerer should give to the crown princess, but a bow that one might give to one of Taliya's cousins—more distant to the throne. That small action stabbed like a knife through her heart, and Taliya narrowed her eyes at him. She wanted to slap him, to scream at him until he acknowledged her as his ruler, but it wouldn't do any good. Tears pricked her eyes in both humiliation and rage. She nodded her head sharply to him and strode out of the room.

The further she walked down the corridor, the angrier she felt. Her fists clenched at her sides. She didn't need Craelyn's help. She *would* find out what Sorcerer Maddoux meant about the children. And gods help her, she would not let anyone stop her.

11

"I have but one final rule to leave you with. Love me. So long as you love me I will never truly be absent. I will return to you soon, my children. See that you follow my ways and you will never regret it." - Berech, from the book of Berech's Law

"Are you ready?" the queen asked, smoothing invisible wrinkles from Taliya's dress.

"Of course, Mother."

"Then stand up tall and smile, dear. The people are *happy* to see you returned to us." She frowned as she glanced at Taliya's scar, then averted her eyes.

King Allandrex shifted from foot to foot, his brows furrowed as the trumpeters announced their entrance. "All this pomp and circumstance over these foreigners."

"Who recovered our daughter safely for us," the queen reminded him in a gentle, chiding voice. "Your war Councils can wait for an evening. The people need this."

The king glanced at his daughter, and his expression eased. "Anything for you, Taliya." He reached out for her and, when she approached, kissed her on the forehead in a rare show of affection. "Anything for you."

The trumpeters fell silent and the doors opened. Taliya felt more than heard the hush that came from the already silent audience. She followed her parents in, holding her head up high as she passed her people. She felt their eyes follow her as she took her seat, scrutinizing her condition. Most kept their eyes politely averted from her face—everyone had already heard about the scar the princess now bore—but a few stared openly at her scar and there were some murmurings.

Craelyn, already standing at his place behind the king's chair, also watched her. His face was expressionless. She couldn't meet his eyes for fear that he would see how angry she was with him.

Lord Kade stepped forward. His voice boomed out to the silent crowd.

"I now present Prince Damin Karl Gordan the Second, son of King Gordan and Queen Lila, along with Sir Timan Worne, both of Glenifer. We thank him for his part in the safe return of Princess Taliya Charlestte Amely Kora, daughter of King Allandrex and Queen Charlestte."

The announcer had left off *heiress to the throne of Kilarya* in her title. Taliya wondered if anyone else noticed the difference. Most of the courtiers seemed too focused on the Gleniferite prince to notice. Taliya wasn't sure whether it was him being Gleniferite, a prince, or handsome that had everyone—specially the women—eyeing him closely. In any case, she was glad that he drew the hungry gaze of the courtiers from her, at least for the moment.

Taliya took two of the three silver balls from the manservant who presented them to her. She stepped down three steps until she was at eye level with Damin, as protocol demanded. She presented them both with the gift, offering a smile. Tim returned her smile, but Damin refused to meet her eyes. Taliya tried not to be hurt.

"I now present Sir Quand W'len, honoured knight of our neighbouring country, Imasdan. We thank him for his part in the safe return of Princess Taliya Charlestte Amely Kora, daughter of King Allandrex and Queen Charlestte."

Sir Quand gave her a deep nod when she presented him with his gift, but he looked uncomfortable. Taliya went back to stand next to her mother, who rose to her feet along with her father.

"And on such a wonderful day of celebration, we have even more delightful news to announce," the queen announced.

Taliya heard a collective inhale from the expectant courtiers, and their attention once again turned to Taliya. There was only one reason the queen would be making an announcement rather than the king or the herald. Taliya felt a flush creep up her cheeks. She wasn't ready for this. She wasn't.

Queen Charlestte beamed and reached over to take Taliya's hand, pulling her forward to stand beside her. Taliya gritted her teeth and twisted her lips into an imitation of a smile.

"Our daughter is now betrothed to Prince Alastar of the Isles of Aminthia! May Berech grace them with many children and even more years of happiness together. Let this mark a time of unity between our two countries!"

The crowd cheered and whistled, but there were a few murmurs of confusion as well. The Queen had been deliberately ambiguous about Taliya traveling to Aminthia, and had left out the part entirely about Milahny being the new heiress.

One thing at a time, Taliya thought to herself. *I suppose they don't want to shock the people too much at once.*

The queen and then the king both stepped forward and kissed her cheek, then bowed their heads politely over her hand. No longer a child and a princess; now she was betrothed and to become a queen. When they stepped back in their place, Taliya offered a deep curtsy of respect to her parents, then the courtiers.

Once most of the cheering and applause had died down, the king nodded, and then both he and the queen hooked arms and strode down the carpet into the next room. After an awkward pause, Damin walked up the steps and offered his arm to Taliya. She accepted, and they followed her parents. Damin stared straight ahead, his mouth tight and his walk stiff. Taliya leaned away from him. Unaware of her discomfort, the people following murmured in excitement at the banquet that was about begin.

The great hall—normally the student hall during the learning months— had been rearranged to fit the raindrop shaped banquet table. The king and queen sat at the central point, the pecking order when down from there. Craelyn was glowering on the king's right, his distaste for social gatherings evident in his eyes. Or maybe it was his distaste for foreigners that she was seeing.

Damin, as Prince of Glenifer, sat beside Taliya. Juliette sat beside Prince Damin on his other side, as Taliya's official escort, and Quand and Tim sat next to her. The rest of Taliya's friends had to sit at the far end with the other students, separated from them by courtiers. Taliya thought she spotted Bryndan and Allec among the pages scurrying about to serve drinks and food to the court. She was grateful that their punishment—whatever it had been—hadn't banned them from serving at the banquet.

"Taliya, how wonderful! Congratulations!" Juliette said. Juliette, of course, already knew about the betrothal as Taliya had talked to her about it almost immediately. Those that heard Juliette also murmured their congratulations to her and Taliya's face heated. Juliette gave Taliya a sympathetic smile, then graciously directed the attention away from her friend.

"Sir Quand, may I ask what brings you to our country?" Juliette's voice was light. Sir Quand was seated next to Juliette, followed by Tim.

"I've come here to help with the training of the pages, Lady…?"

"Juliette. I am Lady Juliette." She awkwardly presented her hand sideways, smiling coyly, and the knight inclined his head over it.

"An honour, Lady Juliette," Sir Quand said.

Taliya fidgeted as Juliette blushed.

"And Prince Damin, it's an honour to meet you as well," Juliette murmured, turning towards him. The coy smile grew brighter as she eyed him.

Taliya felt as if she'd swallowed a bone, her chest was so tight. She didn't want her friend flirting with Damin. Taliya may have been pretty, but Juliette was beautiful.

Damin offered her a polite nod. He glanced at Taliya, and then returned his eyes to his meal. Juliette, looking past Damin, saw Taliya's face. She turned her attentions back to the knight on her left. However, Taliya couldn't help but notice that her friend kept glancing at the pages serving them. Or rather, at one particular page who was serving them. But if Bryndan noticed Juliette's looks, he kept his attention focused on serving the food and drink.

"Sir Quand, perhaps you might enlighten us with a few of your travelling tales?" Juliette said. A few of the courtiers overheard and murmured in agreement.

Quand smiled.

"Stories I have a plenty, but I'm afraid I'm not such a storyteller as Sir Tim."

"Oh?" Juliette turned to look at Tim, who laughed.

"Barding is in my bloodlines, Lady," Tim said. "I haven't done such deeds as Sir Quand, but my ole knight commander had more than a few adventures, and I have a story or two I could tell you about him."

"Oh, yes please!" Juliette clapped her hands together in excitement.

Tim launched into another tale of Lord Staro.

Taliya was grateful for the stories. She didn't feel much like talking to anyone. Damin, she could see, appeared to be of the same mindset. He focused his attention between Tim and his meal, but never once did he open his mouth to speak.

Taliya's eyes strayed to her parents, who were deep in discussion with Craelyn. The sorcerer noticed her attention and looked over at her, his expression bland. Taliya looked away.

The princess counted the minutes until she could leave. At just five courses, the feast was small, but Taliya felt as if it would never end. Just when Taliya was starting to despair that she would have to endure the night for eternity, her parents retired, signalling that the formal gathering was over. Within moments, Taliya declared that she too, would retreat to her bed. Juliette prepared herself to follow her friend, but Taliya shook her head. Juliette gave her a grateful smile, then returned her attention to Sir Tim and Sir Quand.

Taliya refused to look at Damin, who had stood to help her out of her seat. Flustered by his attention after he had spent the evening ignoring her, she turned quickly, tripping over the leg of her father's chair. With a cry, Taliya stumbled to the ground, ripping the hem of her gown. Almost immediately, a hand had lifted her back to her feet.

Taliya blinked up at Damin, her face flushing.

"Are you alright, Princess?"

Taliya opened her mouth to reply when she heard a snicker turned into a cough. She flushed with shame as she became aware of the courtiers—and all her friends—witnessing the spectacle with amusement. She realized that she was still clutching onto the prince and snatched her hands away. Gods help her, she must look like a lovesick kitten. Her face on fire, she fled from the room with her dignity in tatters behind her. She hadn't gone far down the corridor when she heard laughter echoing from the banquet hall. Taliya examined her gown. It was ruined. She closed her eyes against the tears.

12

"This so-called sword, Elishalak, appears to be a myth. It has not been seen since the days of Berech and rumour surrounding it has only grown more spectacular. I believe that Elishalak is a symbol—a metaphor, if you will—for the battle of power that men fight." - From 'Of Prophecies and Myths,' written by Lord Kade.

Quand had already sent two letters to his king all but begging him to return. The situation in Glenifer was grim, and Quand was no spy. Surely there were knights better equipped than him for this task. But the king had yet to reply to his missives, and Quand knew better than to return home against orders.

Lack of experience. When he was a young squire, the knight he served was the sole voice of dissent when Quand had petitioned to gain his knighthood early for that very reason. But Quand, being headstrong and proud, hadn't listened to his knight commander's advice. He was double the fool now; the only difference was that people respected him for it. Had he possessed more experience, he might have known to refuse his king's offer to be champion. All Quand had seen at the time was the glory; he hadn't thought about the political ties that accompanied the post. The political ties that had begun to feel like a noose tightening around Quand's neck.

"Sir Quand?" the voice from the doorway quavered.

The knight's gaze snapped towards the intruder.

"What is it?" he barked.

The servant girl curtsied, her knees quivering. "Lord Jeo is requesting your presence. At the training grounds, sir," she added when he didn't react.

"Brawynn curses! I lost the time." He leapt to his feet with the swiftness of a cat and strode off just as quietly.

The morning light had just started to kiss the ground when Quand strode through the gardens. The training grounds they would use this morning were outside the outer wall, beyond the stables. He ignored the sound of quiet arguing from the gardeners.

At the training grounds, Quand sized up the boys he was to teach. Pages weren't usually required to train before breakfast, but they had to make up for the time lost in the search for the princess. Lord Jeo stepped up and clasped Quand's wrist.

"I'm honoured you joined us, Sir Quand," he teased.

"Ha! As if I'd leave these boys to suffer your instruction."

Jeo's face broke into a smile, a rare occurrence on his scar-worn features.

The knight cast his eyes over the boys. Some had talent, but most would have to work hard to achieve any of the skills. Quand felt the tension in his shoulders ease, as it always did when he got away from the palace walls. This was what he knew; this was where he belonged. He selected the boy nearest him and indicated for the boy to step forward from the line.

"Show me the axyl dance," he commanded.

*   *   *

Taliya slammed the book down and cursed softly.

"Is that any way to treat knowledge?"

She jumped, then turned towards Lord Kade, who was staring at her with raised eyebrows, his arms laden with books.

"Lord Kade, no sir, I'm sorry. I just… never mind." Flustered, Taliya rose to leave, but then paused.

She turned back to her history teacher, who was settling himself into one of the library chairs with a sigh of satisfaction.

"Lord Kade?"

"Hmm?" He settled the books on the table and snagged the top one for himself.

"Is there… do you know if there are any books about my royal lineage?"

Lord Kade looked up at her. Taliya had not been a student to frequent the libraries often.

"For what purpose?"

Taliya shrugged, trying to slow her racing heartbeat.

"I'm curious about my heritage. I'd like to learn more about the royal family."

Lord Kade sighed. He removed his glasses and rubbed his eyes.

"That is regrettable indeed. I'm afraid the King and Queen loaned a number of books on Kilarya to Glenifer. They've probably all been burned by now. What a senseless waste." Lord Kade shook his head, and his eyes teared up. "All that knowledge."

"Is that usual? For Kilarya to send books to other countries?"

Lord Kade frowned. "It's not common, but it does occur on occasion. Usually there is a formal request and your parents hold a Council meeting to discuss which books to send and which to keep. But it was shortly after Lord Maddoux passed away and everyone was grieving. I didn't know it had happened until much later, and to request the books back would have been seen as an insult to Glenifer."

Shortly after Lord Maddoux had passed away was when Craelyn came to power. Maybe there was something in those books that her parents hadn't wanted him to find. Or maybe it was a coincidence and Taliya was just looking for a way to find fault with the sorcerer after the way he had treated her. Taliya ran a hand through her hair, thinking hard.

"What a shame indeed, Lord Kade. Excuse me, please."

Lord Kade rose and bowed to her before settling back into his chair. Taliya went outside to clear her head. Juliette and her friends would likely be at the arena, watching the pages practice. It was a favourite past time of the girls when they got the chance between classes.

As she had suspected, she spotted her friends at the arena and made her way over to them. She raised an eyebrow when she saw Pash.

"Pash, I'm surprised you're out here," Taliya remarked as she approached the group. "The last time you were invited out to join us, I'm fairly certain you said that you had no interest in watching – what was it you said? 'A bunch of boys sweat and grunt as they try to hit each other with sticks'?"

A few girls tittered uncertainly, glancing between Taliya and Pash.

"Oh, *please*." The Gleniferite waved her hand dismissively, her voice almost a purr. "Damin *insisted* I come watch him practice. We had the *best* time catching up on old times in the Gleniferite court. We were friends there, as I may have mentioned."

Juliette looked at Taliya and rolled her eyes. Ever since Damin had arrived, Pash took every opportunity to be near him. When she wasn't around the prince, she could talk of nothing else. Taliya tried to pretend it didn't bother her.

"*Good* friends," Pash continued. "And it would have been something more if my father hadn't taken us out of court. But now that he's *here*, and we're together again…" Pash sighed lusciously.

Taliya gritted her teeth.

Stascha clapped her hands together in excitement. "And maybe soon Prince Alastar will be here as well." She winked at Taliya, who flushed.

Taliya had heard from her parents yesterday that King Jastar had refused to allow Taliya to travel to Aminthia without showing his future daughter-in-law the proper respect. He was instead organizing an entire retinue—lead by none other than Prince Alastar—to come and collect her and escort her back to Aminthia. They would be arriving by mid-summer at the latest, shortly after the summer festival. Taliya knew it was meant to be an honour, but she also wished the spring would never end.

Stascha's comment started a cascade of giggling and speculating among the girls. Taliya moved away from the group to watch the pages on the far side of the arena. She was a little surprised to find a scattering of knights watching the boys as well.

"It's soon time to pick apprentices, Highness," an older knight explained to her after a respectful bow. "The Choosing Ceremony lies shortly after the summer festival, and that is coming soon enough."

She raised her eyebrows at him. "So young?"

"We normally wait until their 16th year, but there is a lot of unrest and we may need them battle ready before too long."

"Because of Glenifer?"

The knight shrugged. "We get more refugees every day. People are doing fine when the weather is warm and there is plenty to share, but if the civil war continues and refugees continue over the border past summer… well, that is a lot of spare mouths to feed and people to shelter and clothe come winter when resources can be scarce. And we need a stronger presence at the border, to make sure Glenifer's civil war doesn't spill over onto us."

"Do you think we will go to war?" Taliya asked.

The knight frowned and rubbed his chin, his eyes still on the pages. "I'm a man of the people and a servant to my king. I let your father worry about the politics and I worry about being the best man I can be to serve up justice to them that needs it. But I will say, if we do go to war, I doubt it will be as short and straightforward a war as we had with Aminthia last year."

That 'war' had ended in a cease-fire after a fortnight.

While they had been talking, a few other knights had gathered around. Taliya heard one mutter, "Too bad our marriage alliance isn't with Imasdan."

"Excuse me?" She turned to search out the speaker, but no one would make eye contact with her.

The knight she had been speaking with cleared his throat. "We all look forward to the upcoming marriage alliance between us and the Isles, Highness. Their navy is a formidable force." But their foot soldiers weren't. Aminthia's army was only trained for war at sea, and any war against Glenifer would be fought over land. Had Taliya been betrothed to an Imasdain prince, the combined forces of the two armies might be enough to dissuade Glenifer from going to war with Kilarya.

"Too bad it's not legal for me to marry *two* different princes," Taliya told the group sarcastically.

There was a short pause, and then the knights roared with laughter. One clapped Taliya on the back as he guffawed.

"You should be a knight, princess. You've already faced more battles than most squires, and you've got the trophy to prove it!" He meant her scar.

For the first time, Taliya felt proud of it. She *had* been in a battle and come out alive. She glanced at the pages. What they were doing didn't look so difficult. What would Bryndan have done if he had been in Taliya's position against those men? She had fought them but hadn't been able to escape. Maybe if she had Bryndan's training, she could have escaped without Damin's help. Her life was fraught with dangers, and marrying into a foreign court would not help her. But maybe Taliya wouldn't have to be so helpless if there was a next time.

She excused herself from the knights, who were still grinning from her joke. Taliya returned to her friends, clustered under a shady willow.

"You've got that look in your eye." Juliette frowned.

Taliya started. "I'm sorry?"

"Don't feign innocence! I know that look. You're planning something and that look on your face says it's something you shouldn't be doing."

Taliya laughed. "You're such a mother hen!"

"Don't do it Taliya. I mean it." Juliette's face was serious.

"Do what, oh beloved friend of mine?" Taliya teased.

"Whatever you're planning. Don't do it."

"How do you know I shouldn't do it if you don't even know what it is?" Taliya asked lightly.

"Because I know *you,* Taliya, and that's enough to worry me. Pray, tell me you won't follow through with whatever foolish plan you were forming. The last time you had that look we followed you into the forest, and look how *that* turned out. We were lucky we didn't get punished—and the boys only got a slap on the wrist. But really, Taliya, you could have *died*."

"Oh, Juliette, it's fine. I'm not about to do something so foolish again. I promise."

Juliette looked about to argue, but the arvile bell interrupted, ringing out the fourteenth hour. The girls hustled off to their riding class, Juliette scowling the whole way. They saddled their horses quickly and hurried out to meet Lady Haley, the horse mistress.

Lady Haley was, as always, wearing a hooded cloak that covered her wild blonde hair. Gossips whispered that the eccentric horse mistress had been kicked in the head by a horse when she first came to teach at the palace and had never been the same since. None of these rumours, however, had deterred the king from keeping her as their horse mistress. She was the only lady who lived outside the palace, in a little house in the village. Taliya had walked past it a few times out of curiosity and always saw at least a few horses crowding the small garden, although there was no gate to keep them in.

"Ladies, to your mounts," Lady Haley ordered from the centre of the arena.

"Pity she's back today," Juliette murmured to Taliya as they mounted. "I was enjoying watching the pages in the arena."

Taliya smiled at her friend, accepting the unspoken peace offering. "I saw your eyes on Bryndan!" Taliya teased. Juliette blushed.

"No more than your eyes were on Allec!" she retorted.

Taliya laughed.

"It *is* a pity she's back," Taliya agreed, returning to Juliette's original comment. "Only gone one day this time. She's doing well."

"It's a wonder your father keeps her employed at all."

Lady Haley interrupted their conversation. "Bring your horses to a trot. And I want to see some good posting for once. Try not to fall off your horses this time!"

Stascha blushed at the directed comment.

Taliya nudged Holjack into a trot, bringing him in to line with the other girls so that they circled the perimeter of the corral. Juliette wasn't wrong about Lady Haley. It *was* a wonder her father kept her employed. Aside from being the only courtier who lived in the village, she was also known to disappear about once or twice a month for a few days at a time. There was no notice given—the girls (or pages) would show up for their horseback riding lesson only to find that she was absent. After a day or two, she would return with no apology and no explanation. She would just continue on as if she had never been gone.

"Stiffer back, Andreia," Lady Haley called. "Just because your seat is moving is no reason not to have proper posture. Juliette, take over the lead from Taliya. She is looking anxious to bring her horse to a gallop. Taliya, don't lean so far forward, dear, not on a trot."

Juliette brought up her dappled horse to take over the lead from Taliya. She smiled apologetically as she passed. Taliya didn't care—Juliette was by far the best rider of the group—but Holjack laid his ears back.

"Stascha, that's wonderful," Lady Haley continued without pause. "You've improved so much."

Taliya could almost feel the other girl's sunny smile from the back of the line.

Holjack stopped in his tracks and turned his ears towards the forest. Without warning, he broke from the circle and headed straight for the woods, picking up speed as he approached the fence.

Lady Haley was watching them with a small smile on her face.

Crazy woman, Taliya thought. She tugged on the reins but Holjack merely shook his head and surged forward. Taliya threw her weight into the stirrups and leaned back with all her might, just as Holjack was bunching his muscles in preparation to jump the fence.

Holjack screamed and reared backwards and Taliya tumbled from the saddle. She ducked her head and rolled, throwing up her arms to protect her head from Holjack's hooves. Somehow, he managed to avoid her. Taliya rolled to a stop, her heart hammering in her chest as she tried to catch her breath.

Taliya took deep, wheezing breaths as she tried to get her bearings and do a mental check for injuries. Holjack whinnied and nuzzled Taliya's face. When Taliya could breathe again—and after determining the only thing wounded was her pride—she rolled onto all fours and Lady Haley helped her to her feet with strong arms. The other girls watched her from their horses with wide eyes.

"I'm fine, I'm not hurt," Taliya assured them. Her face burning with embarrassment; she hadn't fallen off a horse in years.

"You should trust your horse more, Taliya. I've trained Holjack well—he'll always take you where you need to go."

Taliya stared at the horse mistress for a couple of heartbeats. "I didn't think jumping the fence and heading for the woods was a part of today's lesson," she said finally.

Lady Haley threw back her head and laughed, though Taliya didn't feel it was that funny.

"Take Holjack back to the stables and check on him, please," she told Taliya. "No need to come back to the arena today—by the time you brush him down and assess for injuries we'll be almost done."

Taliya gave a slight curtsy of acknowledgement, grateful for the excuse not to face the other girls. Perhaps Lady Haley knew that she needed time to gather the tattered remains of her dignity.

Taliya led Holjack to the stable stiffly. She would have bruises by nightfall.

"What *were* you thinking, eh?" she asked Holjack, scratching his neck as they walked back. "Sometimes I think you're as crazy as Lady Haley."

*   *   *

The staff whistled down. Bryndan blocked it with his own, a hand span before it smashed his head. Without warning, the other end swung around to smack the back of his knees.

Bryndan fell to the ground with a gasp. Again, his opponent's staff plunged towards his head. Bryndan reached up, desperate to block it, but it was a ploy. Bryndan felt the butt of the staff smash into his exposed stomach before he had time to react. He doubled over in agony as tears came to his eyes. He couldn't breathe. Bryndan dropped his own staff and clutched his stomach. Too late he heard his opponent's staff whistling towards his head in a blow that would crush his skull.

"No!"

Bryndan felt a strong arm haul him to his feet as he gasped for air. He looked up at Lord Jeo, his teacher.

"You don't use a kloy block on a stira attack, Bryndan! Use that mulish head, boy."

"But he's just learning that move, sir," Bryndan's opponent, Allec, spoke up. Bryndan shot him a grateful look; it was not easy to stand up to Lord Jeo.

"Do I see a squire's band on you?" Jeo snapped.

Allec dropped his eyes, rubbing his hands over his staff as his face reddened. "No, sir."

"Then by what authority do you even *question* me?"

Allec bowed, eyes on the ground. Jeo held out his hand and Allec gave him his staff.

"You are finished here. Go practise with Trelk. I want to see positions one to eight with swords and their counters. Absolutely *no* variations from them, unlike last time."

Allec bowed again to Lord Jeo's command before heading to the far end of the field.

Bryndan couldn't help but glance at the practise sword that always hung around Allec's waist. He wouldn't receive his own until he was in his final year of pagehood.

"He's a good lad, that boy," Jeo grunted as Allec sauntered away. "He's more driven than most. *He'll* do our country proud."

Jeo's pointed comment wormed into Bryndan, who fought to keep his facial expression impassive.

Emotions were a sign of weakness.

Jeo's attention snapped back to Bryndan. He flipped up the staff that Allec had left behind, nodding for Bryndan to pick up his.

"With the stira attack arcing for the head, it's natural to block with the d'vimi move. Never again let me catch you use the kloy block again for anything, you understand? That's the lazy man's way out. You see how it exposes your stomach? Did you notice how easy it was for Allec to catch you?" He mimed it out for Bryndan. "Do you understand?"

"But, sir, why do we even learn the kloy block if we're never supposed to use it?"

The lord's mouth twitched, but his eyes remained exasperated. "Because it's a learning tool, lad. Now enough yammering. I'm not paid to make you into a lazy knight. Yames!"

This last was bellowed with such force that Bryndan jumped. He looked across the arena to the tall, lean page. As Yames climbed off his opponent's head and ambled over, the other boy scrambled to get up, coughing dust. He scuttled away, presumably to find a more manageable partner.

"Yes, sir?"

Jeo tossed the staff to Yames, who caught it without breaking eye contact.

"Stira attack, 50 times. Don't take it too slow. Even short warriors don't wait for you to catch your breath in a battle." Bryndan flushed. He *hated* when people commented on his size. "Once that's done, you can go back to wrestling. Bryndan, the crown can't afford a lazy knight. Ten laps around the field before you leave here today."

"Lord Jeo-"

"Twenty laps, then. Not another word."

Bryndan opened his mouth again but Yames, twirling the staff to get its measure, somehow managed to jam it into Bryndan's ribs and wind him before he could speak. Both boys bowed as Jeo marched off to watch the others train.

"Don't you ever learn?" Yames hissed once Jeo was far enough away. "I can't believe you talked back. Have I taught you nothing in our years together as fosterlings?"

Bryndan shrugged. "It's not fair!"

"Bryndan, shut up. No one cares. It's not like you're any worse off than the other boys, and nobody likes a whiner."

"I wasn't whining!" Bryndan protested, his voice rising.

Yames raised his eyebrows.

"I was standing up for my rights- "

"What rights? In case you've forgotten, Bryndan, you're a page. You have no rights."

"This isn't a hen house!" Jeo yelled. Both boys cringed. "Practise your drills before the lesson is over."

Jeo didn't need to add a threat. Both boys stepped into position.

"Guard!" Yames said as he lunged into the attack. Bryndan barely saved himself from a whack across his head.

"*In Berech's name.* Give me more notice, will you?"

"Would your enemies give you notice?" Yames retorted.

Bryndan's arms were aching afterwards from the constant impact of Yames's staff, but he pursed his lips without complaint. Complaining was a sign of weakness.

"Have fun with the laps. I'll talk to you later." Yames clapped him on the shoulder.

"Yeah, sure, thanks," Bryndan muttered, grimacing.

"It's not Eliva's bane, Bryndan. You'll survive. You're not the strongest or brightest one in the arena, but your stubbornness could rival a brawynn's."

Bryndan glared at Yames, but the taller boy had already turned away. Now that he had a moment to himself, Bryndan's thoughts turned inward. It had always been his birthright to be a knight, but it wasn't until he had ventured out with Taliya and the others into the woods that he realized how much he *wanted* it. Things might have turned out differently then if he had been better trained. Taliya might never have fallen into the river. They might have returned triumphant together, rather than racing back on horseback to get help from the castle.

They'd had four new students join their classes this week, refugees from Glenifer. Bryndan didn't just want to speak with them in classes and make them feel welcome; he wanted to go out and *help* them. The roads were dangerous, and not everyone who made it out of Glenifer arrived at Korign. And if he were out of the castle, maybe he wouldn't be thinking so much about Taliya. The news of her betrothal shouldn't have come as a surprise, but it cut him all the same. He hadn't dared ask her how she felt about it—their friendship didn't tread on such sensitive ground. Bryndan somehow didn't think she was all that happy about it. *He* wouldn't want to be forced to marry. As fourth born son to a lowly country lord, that was not going to be his burden in life. He would have the liberty to travel as a knight and settle when—or if—he chose.

Bryndan glanced around the arena. Everybody was gone. He slowed to a walk, breathing deep. How long had he been out here? He hustled over to the stables, where the next class had already started. He did not see Prince Damin sitting on the fence, watching him with narrowed eyes.

13

"Remember that time belongs to Mother Jualis and not to man. Have patience, and never relax your guard." – Imasdan Proverb

Taliya lit a candle in the temple, then looked around to see if some miraculous sign would occur. A ground tremble or a crack of thunder would have sufficed. But if the gods *were* aware of Taliya's presence —and her role in the prophecies—they were silent.

She approached one of the stained-glass windows and looked at the inscription below it. The prophecies were why she was here. She had asked Lord Kade about the Elyan prophecies, but he had frowned and told her she was *much* too young to understand them, and she should focus on more important matters—such as the steady flow of refugees to Kilarya. She had started searching through the library, but after Craelyn crossed her path twice in a row there, she didn't feel it was safe anymore. She didn't want him to know that she was still trying to learn what Lord Maddoux had meant about the children not being children. Well, that and about her heritage—to try and uncover why she might not be a suitable queen for Kilarya— and those strange voices claiming her Elyan. Taliya almost wished she didn't have classes and royal duties to attend, as her research was eating up most of her spare time and getting her nowhere.

So, here she was at the temple, feeling desperate.

"Taliya?"

Taliya jumped, then closed her eyes in embarrassment.

"What are you doing here?" The words came out sharper than she had intended.

Damin's eyes crinkled in a smile. "I could ask you the same question. I didn't think you spent much time in the temples."

Taliya flushed. "I could say the same thing about *you*."

Damin's smile widened.

"Peace, Taliya. I wanted a quiet place to think. The temple is always a place that welcomes visitors—and silence."

"Oh, I'm sorry. I didn't… I mean, I hadn't come here to intrude."

"I didn't think you had."

"Oh." Taliya felt flustered, and her face grew hotter. "Where's Tim?"

"I believe he's doing some sword practice. I promised him I wouldn't wander far."

"Oh," Taliya said again. Then she blurted, "I came here to learn more about Elyan."

Damin's gaze sharpened. "Because of Raspin."

Taliya didn't disagree.

A temple guardian approached. He nodded his head in respect, but did not bow. It would be unbecoming for a speaker of the gods to bow to any human.

"May I help you?"

Taliya turned to him. "I would like to hear more about the Elyan prophecies."

"Of course. I would be delighted to answer your questions if I can."

When both Damin and the temple guardian looked at her expectantly, Taliya hesitated. Somehow, she had thought the guardian would just spill forth with knowledge and information. She was so lost she didn't know what to start asking.

"Um…" Taliya glanced around the temple and her eyes fell on the writing beneath the stained glass.

"What is the inscription below this image?"

"It's in ancient Kilaryan, one of the purest translated verses we have relating to the Elyan prophecies. In common language, it reads:

Never forget
Eliva's Child of destruction and hope
Worlds will clash, burn, fall, and shadow
Will one to die.
One choice have you to make this day of endless night
Ring out your sacrifice!
Let go your hope, freedom, powers to release eternity
Die all if failed.

"Oh," Taliya said. She glanced at Damin, who was watching her with an expression she couldn't fathom. She looked back at the temple guardian. "Do you know what it means?"

"Our scholars have studied the prophecies for years and know that in the end times Elyan—referred to as Eliva's Child here—will rise to power and bring Berech back to us, that he may save us from destruction of the Alirth Clash."

Damin snorted. The temple guardian frowned and turned to look at him.

"Actually, I believe scholars can *theorize* over prophecies but not *prove* them. Proving prophecies is a right reserved to Jualis and Kilmar."

"Are you mocking the gods, the prophecies, or myself?" His voice was cold.

"You worship Berech as a god, but he's just a man. You risk angering Jualis, Mother Sun of Light, and Kilmar, Father Universe of Life. Perhaps they will come down and smite this country for blasphemy."

The guardian drew himself up, his face furious.

"What's the 'Alirth Clash?'" Taliya asked hastily with a warning glance to Damin. She didn't want to offend the guardian; she was here for answers.

The guardian took a deep breath and turned to look at her, turning his shoulders to cut Damin from his view. Damin snorted again and wandered off to another area of the temple. Taliya's shoulders relaxed.

"The Alirth Clash is the last battle of our world—when Eliva clashes with a shadow planet. It is said that Berech will be the determining factor in whether Eliva is saved or consumed."

Taliya frowned. *Shadow planet.* The voices in the woods had spoken to her of shadow planets.

"Is a shadow planet like a parallel world?" Taliya asked.

The guardian rocked onto his heels, warming up to the subject as he appeared to forget about Damin completely. "Shadow planets are just as their name says; two worlds existing side-by-side in different universes, but with a strong bond connecting them. They *shadow* one another. While there can be thousands of parallel worlds in any given space, shadow planets come in pairs. Another big difference between shadow planets and parallel worlds is that it has been theorized that every shadow planet pair will eventually clash with one another. That is, they draw too close together for both to exist. When this happens, one world will absorb the other and either one or both worlds will be destroyed." He looked at Taliya's face and smiled. "Don't worry. It will likely be centuries before that happens; first, Elyan will appear and warn us."

"Could it be wrong—what the prophecies say about Elyan? Maybe Elyan won't come at the end of the world? Or... maybe it could be changed?"

The temple guardian shook his head. "Prophecies are impossible to change. It *cannot be done.* But I suppose they can be misinterpreted—unlikely, but possible."

Taliya's head spun and the start of a headache was pricking behind her eyes. She thanked the temple guardian, who nodded and walked away.

Taliya left the temple deep in thought. Damin fell into step beside her, but she didn't feel like talking to him.

They walked in silence for a few moments, then Damin grabbed her elbow to stop her. She turned to face him.

"You better not go on about your precious 'Berech' to your delectable fiancé," he snapped. "The Aminthians believe him to be a false prophet who enslaved our world. They also believe that Elyan will liberate us from Berech's oppression. If they think Raspin is truly Elyan, they will join the wrong side of the war. If they think he's a false prophet, they will seek him out to burn him—and they will kill any of his followers."

"And to what do I owe such a courteous warning?" Taliya snapped back, clenching her fists. "If this is how you choose to speak to me, pray, go back to ignoring me!"

Damin dropped her elbow and stepped back as if she'd slapped him. His face was unreadable as he stared at her.

"I wasn't... I wouldn't..." he paused, flustered, then bowed and strode ahead of her.

Taliya couldn't understand him. It was like she kept seeing two different men in the same skin: the kind, attentive one from the forest, and the short-tempered, snappy one from the palace.

She wanted to run after him; she wanted to scream at him and punch him. She turned and stomped to the riverbank. What she *really* wanted, she decided, was to scream and punch whoever had decided to make her think she was a prophet. The *real* Elyan would be wise and powerful, more like perfect Milahny or the legendary Sir Quand. Elyan wouldn't have stupid reoccurring nightmares about being burned alive. Elyan wouldn't... Taliya hiccoughed. Elyan wouldn't be trembling at the thought of facing the end of the world. *The Alirth Clash.* What was it? When was it coming... or, had it already started? Taliya picked up a rock and hurled it into the river.

*   *   *

Taliya paced in the small, sparse chamber. She massaged her finger where her ring used to be. What if he didn't come? What if he *did* come? Would he mock her? Tell her father? What if-

The door creaked open and Taliya froze. Could someone else have found... but it was him. She offered a tense smile and he bowed in response. Taliya opened her mouth but couldn't seem to find her voice. She swallowed twice, then tried clearing her throat. It came out as a squeak.

He half rose from his bow to glance at her. "You requested my presence, Highness."

"Page Allec, yes, I did. I sent you a note. I see you got it. Thank you, yes, thank you. Come in, please." Taliya cleared her throat again, her face burning. Could he see how much she was blushing in this light?

"Please, sit down, Page Allec."

Taliya perched in one of the chairs, offering the other to him with a wave.

He pulled the chair further away before he sat. Taliya saw him glance twice to the door and realized that she was not the only one who was nervous. And why not? After all, she was betrothed to Prince Alastar of the Isles of Aminthia and had the audacity to call Allec into a secret meeting without escort. Taliya cursed herself for not thinking this through more carefully. If they were caught, it would be Allec who bore the brunt of the punishment. And yet he had come as she had asked. She felt hopeful he would help her.

"I've called you here because... because I need your help. Again."

"I don't recall a happy ending to the last time I helped you," Allec said dryly. "I'm still washing dishes, you know."

Taliya wasn't sure if he was serious or teasing. She chose to ignore his comment.

"What I am to ask you isn't... well, it's not against the law, but it isn't exactly permitted, either."

Allec sucked in a breath and shifted his chair back further, glancing again at the door. His hands twitched as if he were preparing to bolt. Taliya flushed. She was making this worse.

"I need you to train me how to fight!" Taliya blurted. She bit her lip, waiting for his reaction.

Allec frowned in confusion, but he also stopped looking at the door.

"I've read through the laws carefully, Allec. It is not against Kilaryan law for a woman to be taught to fight. But what man would teach any woman—let alone me—to do so?" Taliya offered a crooked smile.

"Why me? Why not someone with more skill, like a squire or a knight?"

Taliya shrugged. "When we were in the woods together, you were so in control, so certain of yourself. I've watched you fight on the grounds, and you're the best page there is. The squires rarely leave their knight's side. And again, what knight would train me?"

"I hear Imasdan has a lady knight in its ranks." Allec's eyes roamed the small room, avoiding the princess' gaze.

"Allec, Sir Quand is here to train the pages and nothing else. He would never risk it. He *could* never risk it."

"And you believe I could, Princess?" Allec asked.

Taliya was not sure what emotion lay behind his voice.

"You helped me before." Taliya's voice was small. She rubbed her bare ring finger and waited, her heart pounding in her chest. Allec looked at his hands for a few minutes, considering. Finally, he looked back up at her.

"The Choosing Ceremony is less than a season away."

Taliya nodded, uncertain where he was leading.

Allec threw his hands wide in a helpless gesture. "I *can't*, Highness. I can't risk it, especially after what happened to you in the woods. I don't think you understand how close Bryndan and I came to losing our positions here. But I've still been put on notice, and if I step out of line again I'm out *like this*." Allec snapped his fingers. "Even coming here tonight was a risk for me. Please, Taliya, don't command this of me."

His last words echoed in Taliya's mind. Do not *command* this. For a brief moment, she considered doing just that. What would he say if she confessed that she was Elyan? That the true reason she wanted to learn to fight was because she would need to be at her best to face what was coming? Taliya took a breath to speak, then let it out slowly. He would never believe her; at best, he would think her crazy and at worst he may call for her to be burned at the stake. Allec may obey her if she commanded him to do this, but he would never respect her. Taliya was starting to learn that being a good ruler did not mean always getting what you wanted—it meant knowing how much you could ask of your people. With a sigh, she dismissed him.

He left with evident relief and Taliya's heart sank. She had gone through her choices with great care. The only other she felt she could ask was Bryndan, but she had seen him in the arena. While Allec fought as if he had been born with a sword in his hand, Bryndan looked as if he held a drægon's tail. And would it be fair to put the risk on him? He might agree, but would he, like Allec, feel trapped? What sort of ruler would exploit her people for her own benefit?

Taliya sighed in defeat. She had but one option left available to her: she would have to teach herself.

*　　　*　　　*

Trelk stayed off Jeo's training field, but it was at night that Bryndan remained vulnerable. Two nights after Trelk had given up his sword to Jeo, Bryndan had woken to find a knife stabbed into the pillow beside him. Showing his roommates had been a mistake. They had told Lord Jeo, who had approached Trelk. The larger boy claimed innocence and no one could prove otherwise, but everyone knew about the bad blood between them. Later, Bryndan had run into Trelk, who warned him that if Bryndan accused him of anything again, the knife would be in Bryndan's face and not his bed.

Bryndan believed him. And so, in the following days, as he woke up to a bed full of spiders, a live snake, and once a dead cat, Bryndan had held his tongue, disposing of Trelk's gifts before his roommates took notice.

It came to the point that sleeping with one eye open wasn't working at all, so Bryndan chose to not sleep. All his spare time went into preparing for when he would first spar with his training sword. He rose earlier than his roommates and went to bed late at night, if at all. Many of them were too exhausted to notice or care about his constant absences. Bryndan caught up on sleep in spare time, which often meant during meals. His friends teased him, speculating that he was attempting to lose weight for the Summer Festival to dance with the ladies. Bryndan, sensing Trelk's glare, kept his mouth shut and endured the teasing.

His parents occasionally wrote to him from the country, reminding him that the family honour rested on his shoulders and bragging over the exploits of his eldest brother, who was his father's heir. They never asked how he was doing. Bryndan answered every one, even though he hadn't seen his family since he had been sent to be a fosterling at the castle at the age of nine.

The crown required that every noble family offer a son as a fosterling once the boy turned nine. Those that couldn't had to pay an extra tax every year. Almost all the boys who came were third or fourth born and not in a position to inherit the estate. Families waved these sons off with a sense of relief, and the freshly abandoned fosterlings soon developed a new family—a brethren—in their peers and knight commanders. Those who could not handle the rigours of knighthood often stayed in the castle as guards, revoking their titles in preference to remaining in the only home they really knew.

Bryndan clenched his teeth as he began his nightly training routine. He always started with push-ups because he *hated* them. Despite his slow progress, Bryndan felt a glimmer of pride stir within him. Less than a fortnight after the Summer Festival, every page in his final year would spend a day in the arena to demonstrate their skills. Everything from sparring to wrestling to jousting was executed. There was no passing or failing. It was merely a demonstration of skills put on before the knights looking for a squire. Every knight without a squire—if they could be spared—would attend the demonstration. The Choosing Ceremony happened only a month later, but by that time every page chosen for squire already knew which knight he would be serving, and the ceremony was more a formality than anything else.

Bryndan wouldn't be chosen this year as he was still too young, but he would still be expected to put on a demonstration with the others. Still, the demonstration was nothing compared to his obsession over his impending battle against Trelk. The moon was his lantern as he ran laps and practised drill sets with his staff. The weather was warming as spring blossomed and Bryndan curled up in the stables when he was too tired to train. Slim, the stable master, never said anything. But on more than one morning, Bryndan woke with a thick horse blanket tossed over his shoulders.

When it finally occurred to Trelk that Bryndan was no longer reacting to his gifts, he stopped leaving them. Mostly.

14

"The simplest route is not always the easiest." –
Gleniferite Proverb

Taliya grit her teeth in frustration. It looked so simple when
Allec had done this manoeuvre with his sword. She had stolen
one of the staves from the equipment storage. Every sword
would be accounted for, but a staff was less likely to be
missed—especially one that had a deep crack on one side.

Taliya closed her eyes and thought of how she had seen
Allec do it earlier. He had stepped his left foot out and-

"Not a bad rendition of the kloy block," said a man's voice.

Taliya whirled around so quickly she tripped over her feet
and fell onto her backside with a small shriek. Prince Damin
stood at the edge of the clearing, watching her. How long had
he been there? Taliya put a hand to her heart and tried to calm
her breathing. Tim stood a few steps behind his prince. But, for
once, the older man held his tongue. He nodded once to her
and faded back into the shadows. Taliya didn't doubt he would
remain on guard. Her face was burning as she untangled herself
from her staff. How could this man make her feel so clumsy
and stupid?

"Sir," Taliya said. She was about to say something cutting,
but her tongue froze as she thought about what he had said. He
knew what she was doing. Jualis curse him, she was at his
mercy. If Damin ever brought this to her father...

Damin approached her and bowed, holding out his hand.
Taliya grimaced and allowed him to pull her to her feet. She
took meticulous care to brush off every bit of dust from her
clothes, buying herself time to think.

Damin looked amused. "Are you trying to teach yourself to fight?"

Taliya lifted her chin. "What else am I to do? No one would risk teaching me and it seems a practical skill to learn."

"Why? Are you planning any more forays into the woods? Or perhaps you're more concerned about your fiancé?" His last sentence was cutting.

Taliya turned away so he wouldn't see how much his comments had hurt her.

"You wouldn't understand." She said thickly. "I'm so... *helpless.*"

A foolish thing for a princess to say, but Taliya could think of no other word. An heiress rejected from her own throne for reasons she hadn't yet worked out, and a prophet from the end of times who was supposed to... Taliya wasn't even sure what Elyan was supposed to do. Most of the prophecies were untranslated from ancient Kilaryan and Taliya was loathe to appear too interested in it. Craelyn was watching her; she knew it as much as she knew that her ring was in the possession of the drægons. But even if she could prove that Craelyn was observing her, what crime was he actually committing?

Damin stepped closer to her and put his hand on her shoulders to turn her around. He cupped her cheeks with his hands when she was facing him again.

"Aye, Princess. I'm afraid I *do* understand." He sounded sad—more sad than Taliya had ever heard him.

She glanced up at him in surprise. He was watching her gravely. "D'you think I'd have come here had I *any* chance of saving my family? I would've rather died in battle than run away like a coward, but I'm a prince before I'm a knight. Tim reminded me of that." He nodded his head to where Tim had disappeared into the brush.

"Your life is not yours to command," Taliya murmured.

They smiled shyly at each other, sharing an understanding of the other's burden.

Damin cleared his throat, dropping his hand and stepping back. An impish smile lit his face, hiding the vulnerability that she had seen a moment before.

"I, for one, have never been able to follow the rules. Ask Tim! Of all my siblings, I was always the one caught with my hand in the cookie jar—but the cookie was always worth it. I'm a terrible snoop into other peoples' business when I can help it." He bowed. "I'd be honoured to help you learn to fight. And if I'm lucky, maybe I'll get to see you use those skills to help you ward off annoying husbands-to-be when they arrive in court."

Taliya laughed, as he had meant her to. She swung her staff at him in a mock blow and he blocked it easily.

His eyes turned serious again. "Truce?" he asked her.

Taliya knew that he wasn't just talking about this morning. She agreed. She had missed the Damin she had come to know in the woods.

He gestured to her.

"Now, show me that kloy block again. This time widen your feet a bit and hold your hands lower on the grip. You know, it would be easier in trousers than a skirt."

"And when I'm attacked, I'll be sure to ask the men to kindly wait for me to change into trousers." Taliya rolled her eyes. "*Really*, Damin."

"Fair enough. Now, swing that staff from the left, using momentum from your hips."

The following morning, they met in the same place at the southern edge of the gardens, surrounded by trees and shrubbery. Tim had again arrived, nodded, and faded into the darkness. He was more solemn than he had been in the woods.

They met every morning after that. The garden was small and Taliya had suggested that with two people it might be better to train outside the walls in the arena where there was more space, but Damin had flatly refused.

"I don't want to distract anyone else," was all he would say. When pressed on who else would *possibly* be practising before dawn, he had pursed his lips and not answered her question. Taliya had shrugged off his secrecy. The arena was more exposed than the gardens anyway, and she didn't want a guard on night duty to spot her training. *And you're afraid of the forest,* she reminded herself. Funny how she forgot that when Damin was with her. Still, even if Damin stood at her side, it would take a lot more to go back to the forest. There were too many places for robbers to hide.

"Watch my shoulders and torso. No, stop looking at my face. That's your first mistake. The danger is not in my face, but *here*. Do you see?" Taliya nodded, focussing her eyes straight ahead to Damin's chest. It was a cold morning and a dusting of frost covered the ground.

"Now I'm going to mime out a movement for you, and you're going to mime out the defence you would use." Damin stood two paces away from her. As she watched, his left shoulder dropped forward, and his body twisted to the right. At the last second, he dropped to the ground and thrust his right shoulder up, punching his arm slowly towards her. The shadows cast tricky lights on their movements, but Taliya managed to mime the appropriate counter block, equally as slow. They had stopped dressing so warmly now that spring had lost its chill.

"Excellent. Now, we'll do it faster."

"Can't we try it with a weapon now?" she snapped, shivering with cold. Perhaps it wasn't such a warm morning after all.

Damin gave her a patient smile, which made Taliya even more annoyed. He didn't seem so bothered by the chill. "We could. But then your focus would be on the weapon. It's just as easy to fool someone with a weapon as it is with a face. If you learn the moves without the weapon first, you'll know where to look and won't be so easily fooled. I'm teaching your body how to move, and how to react."

"Is this how they teach it in Glenifer?"

"Well, no. They taught us how to use a weapon first and foremost. But trust me; this'll work. You see, by the time I get you to use the staff, you'll be able to spar with anyone."

"If you say so." Taliya grunted. She couldn't believe that she had asked for this.

"I do."

Damin stopped smiling, his dark eyes watching her with an unfathomable expression. Uncomfortable, Taliya looked towards the lightening sky.

"It's nearly dawn," she observed.

"And I need to catch up on some sleep." Damin saluted and took his leave. He walked back through the wooden doors into the castle. He had gone less than ten steps when Tim caught up with him and, after a wave to Taliya, followed his prince inside. Taliya watched them go.

"You shouldn't be doing this," Jef said from behind her in his thick, country accent.

Taliya turned and smiled at him. "Hello, Jef."

The gardener looked worried. "You shouldn't be *doing* this, Princess. I know I may just be a gardener and all, but I think I know more about what's going on than *you* do."

"What do you know, Jef? What's going on?" Taliya's heart pounded in her chest. Was he talking about the prophecy? Did he know about Elyan?

Jef just shook his head. "It's not for a princess to be fighting. And not right for a promised woman to be spending so much time with another man."

Taliya's shoulders sank in relief at his concerns. "Believe me, I don't think Prince Damin and I are in *any* danger of that. He cares nothing for me." Taliya's heart squeezed as she said it, but she brushed her feelings aside.

Jef pressed his lips together and shook his head, then sighed. "But, ah, how are those dreams of yours?" he asked, changing the topic.

Taliya rubbed her head, laughing bitterly. "You know I hardly sleep any more, Jef. I'm too busy training with Prince Damin."

But as she said it, she felt herself being pulled back into her nightmare.

Taliya gasped for breath as smoke filled her lungs, making her choke and cough. The hairs on her arms and legs were scorched from the heat, and the fire raged around her face. The hair on her head had been burned off seconds before and her scalp ached with oozing blisters. She couldn't breathe. Flames licked the wood around her and Taliya stumbled back.

And then she was across the room from herself, watching herself being eaten alive by the flames. Seeing herself scream and reach out a hand in supplication, begging to be saved. But she did not reach out to save the Taliya who was being burned alive; she never did. Instead, she turned and fled from the other Taliya, her cowardice wrapping around her like a snake that devoured her. And blackness reached out and welcomed her, swallowing her into its belly.

The princess gasped and tore herself from the dream's clutches, her chest heaving. She shook herself to be rid of the nightmare and put a hand up to her head, feeling her hair. Something had changed; she had never had the nightmare while awake before. It was getting worse. She missed the comfort of her ring. Her stomach clenched as she thought of the drægons. She had been a fool to trust them.

"The fire…" Taliya looked down at her hands, her voice trembling.

Jef gave her an indecipherable look, as if he knew something that she didn't.

"It's getting late, Highness," he said after a moment's silence.

Taliya bit her lip, clenching and unclenching her fingers. After a moment she sighed and glanced up at him, dropping her hands to her side. "See you tomorrow, Jef."

"As always, Highness, it will be a pleasure." The man bowed and Taliya turned to leave. But as she reached the door, he whispered anxiously, "Don't tell him, Highness. He *will* kill you."

She turned back around, startled, but the gardener had already faded into the darkness. She had an eerie feeling that he wasn't referring to her training, but Jef would never tell her what he meant. She glanced around the gardens, searching out an invisible enemy. The shiver that went down her spine was not caused by the chill alone and Taliya fled back into the warmth of the castle.

*   *   *

Bryndan woke to see an amused face peering at him. He rubbed the sleep from his eyes and sat up slowly, his muscles protesting.

"I too find a stable much more comfortable than my bed," Prince Damin said.

Bryndan shrugged instead of answering the prince. He got to his feet and folded up the blanket that Slim had left him.

"Especially when dead things appear in it," Damin added.

Bryndan gave him a sharp look. "Who said there were dead things in my bed, Prince?"

Damin grinned, which made him look younger. Bryndan remembered that the prince was barely past his youth.

"A bird told me... but it's dead now."

Bryndan shrugged again and started to walk away.

"Hey," Damin called.

Bryndan turned around. "Yes, Prince?"

The smile had dropped from Damin's face and he looked grim. He had pulled out a black swan feather from his pocket and was toying with it.

"What I told you earlier is true: Trelk does want to kill you. I've seen that look before. And he doesn't hate everyone, either. Just you. What in Eliva have you done to earn his enmity?"

Bryndan sighed. The prince was going to find out from one person or another about Bryndan's shame. He might as well tell him and get it over with.

"It's... it's more a family thing."

The prince raised his eyebrows. Bryndan sighed and kicked the dust.

"We live on neighbouring lands. Our fathers have always been squabbling over territory."

"Truly a grievous and unforgivable offense," Damin said sarcastically.

"It's worse. My eldest brother... well, he seduced Trelk's twin sister."

Damin's eyebrows climbed up in his forehead. "And your fathers disagreed with the match?"

"There was no match... she, uh, she learned she was pregnant and... my brother had lost interest at that point. We all knew the baby was his, but he denied it and dragged her name through the mud. So, she..."

Damin swore. "She took her own life?"

"Leena," Bryndan said. "Her name was Leena, and she was 14 years old."

He closed his eyes against the shame. It was one of the reasons why he was so silent and accepting about Trelk's bullying. Because deep down, he felt he deserved to be punished for his brother's crime.

"What happened to your brother?"

"Well, no one could prove my brother was the guilty party. My father argued that the responsible party was a traveling minstrel. Our two families have been rivals for so long that the courts just wanted to wash their hands of us. They ordered my family to pay retribution in the way of giving Trelk's family ownership of the disputed land, and called it even."

Damin whistled. "Kilmar's curse, I would hate you too if I were Trelk."

Damin hesitated and glanced at Tim, who nodded. "Listen, I know about your match. I've been watching him. He's a dirty fighter, and I would expect nothing less from him on the day. He may just have a *slip* of the sword at an opportune moment. Trelk, I mean. If you want a chance at holding your own, or at winning, you'll have to learn more than what Jeo can teach you, little page."

Bryndan hesitated. What the prince was suggesting was against the rules. He chewed on his lip. Damin leaned against the stall door and waited.

"Are you offering to teach me, Highness?"

Damin laughed. "To fight dirty? Nah, it's just a warning. I wouldn't know the first thing about it."

Bryndan sensed that the prince was lying. He rubbed his head and sighed.

"Thank you, Highness, but I couldn't. If I lose my honour, what've I got left?"

"Your life, little page. You'd have your life."

It was tempting, so tempting to agree. Bryndan would need every advantage to defeat Trelk. And the prince was right; Trelk would not restrict himself to fair practise in the arena.

"No," Bryndan said. "I won't win that way. How would I be any different than Trelk if I did?"

Damin was still leaning against the stall, but he was as relaxed as a cat ready to pounce. They stood for a moment in tense silence before Damin pushed his shoulders against the wall to stand upright. He bowed to Bryndan.

"As you like it, little page. I look forward to the match."

The prince turned to go.

"Page Bryndan, Highness," Bryndan said.

Damin turned around, cocking his head to one side.

"I'm Page Bryndan. Not 'little page'."

Damin shrugged. "As you like it."

15

"A true knight makes his own luck." - From Yim Sandish, First Knight of Imasdan

Jeo stood between Bryndan and Trelk. Trelk gave a toothy smile, looking like a drægon on the hunt. He had not stopped smiling since Jeo announced their bout two days before. It was not unheard of for a page in his final year to fight a first-year page in the arena, but it was unusual. So long as the match kept to basic fight patterns and was supervised by two knights, it could happen.

Jeo's announcement had caused a stir within the castle and Bryndan cringed as he saw how many had turned up to watch the match. He did not think he had ever been more terrified in his life—not even when he had watched the princess get swept away in the river Koris. So much had happened since then.

"This is a points match," Jeo said. "A hit anywhere on the arms or shoulders gains one point. A hit on the torso three points. The first person to 10 points wins. When Sir Quand or I call an end to the match, you both step back *immediately* and put down your weapons. If you draw blood on the upper body—excluding the head or neck—it's an automatic win. If you knock your opponent unconscious, it's an automatic win. You must yell 'forfeit' if you wish to quit. And your opponent will *stop fighting and step back*." Jeo paused a half second to give Trelk a hard look. "During the fight, you stick to manoeuvres you learned in training. Swords and wrestling only—no other weapons. Any questions?"

"No, Lord," Trelk and Bryndan murmured. Jeo looked at Quand.

"Witnessed," Quand said.

Jeo nodded to the two boys. "You may commence your warmup. I'll call you into the arena shortly."

Bryndan bowed and walked to the opposite corner of the arena from Trelk. He wanted to throw up. He wiped his sweaty palms on his trousers and began his routine stretches. The other boys crowded around outside the fence. Rules stated that once in the arena, no one could touch either Bryndan or Trelk until after the bout had ended. They yelled and whistled their encouragement instead.

Jeo leaned against one of the posts. Bryndan tried to believe that Jeo was right, that he must face his fears to overcome them. But staring his nightmare in the face made Bryndan wish to run away as fast as he could. He glanced away from his opponent and caught the eye of the princess. He flushed when he realized she was there to watch as well. She gave him a smile of encouragement and nodded. Even from here, Bryndan could see the reddened scar on her face. She had been outnumbered and overpowered by those robbers in the woods, but still she had fought back. Her confidence gave him strength.

Sir Quand called them to the centre of the arena. Bryndan picked up his sword and dragged his feet to where Quand stood. Trelk was already there, prancing about like a warhorse. The older page brought up his sword and Bryndan mimicked the opening gesture.

"Begin!" Quand roared. But Trelk had already started. He attacked Bryndan in a blurred series of swipes and thrusts, which Bryndan managed to block.

Bryndan knew he was in trouble. Trelk used the basic page manoeuvres, but with a flourish that Bryndan had never learned. Bryndan blocked the sideswipe and the following thrust. Trelk attacked with a backhanded parry and a forward thrust and Bryndan dodged both. Barely.

You can't win on defence, a voice mocked in his head. *If you don't attack, Lord Jeo will kick you out of training.* Yet he couldn't attack. Trelk was too fast and strong. Bryndan was weakening already. A flash of metal whipped towards his side. Bryndan dropped and rolled. On his way, he snapped the broad end of his training sword at Trelk's feet. Trelk crashed to the ground with a grunt, but was back on feet within seconds. Bryndan regained his own feet half a heartbeat later.

Trelk's movements blurred as he advanced. He spun his sword, switching his lead food and twisting to the side as he lunged. Bryndan dodged the blade but didn't see Trelk's fist. The larger boy punched him soundly in the shoulder and Bryndan's whole sword arm went numb. Bryndan switched sword hands before he dropped the blade.

"Point!" Jeo yelled.

Trelk lunged again, sensing victory. Bryndan danced to the side, bringing up his blade in a clumsy counter-thrust. Trelk dodged easily and twisted around, his other fist connecting with Bryndan's side.

"Three points, Trelk!" Jeo called.

The twist had put Trelk off balance. As Bryndan flailed back from the blow, his sword caught Trelk in the upper arm, slicing it open.

"First blood!" Allec shouted from the stands.

"Step back!" Quand yelled at the same time.

Bryndan clutched his side, eyes tearing in agony. He gasped like a fish but couldn't remember how to breathe. Through his tears, Bryndan saw Trelk staring down at him in shock and rage. It wasn't a fair win. Both of them knew it. But the rules were clear and fair or not, Trelk had lost. A snarl rose on Trelk's lips. Bryndan took another step away and tripped over his own feet, crashing to the ground.

"For Leena," Trelk shouted, as he swung his sword around and grabbed it with both hands to stab Bryndan with a soldier's blow, meant to execute prisoners. And then Trelk howled, dropping his sword to the ground. He bent in half and clutched his right leg, screaming like a brawynn in its death throes. Jeo tackled Trelk, pinning him to the ground. Trelk continued to howl.

"You shame us all, Trelk." Jeo said. He sounded sad. "We've all witnessed your attempted murder. The tribunal will decide your fate." Jeo shook his head. "You used to be the best of us." He glanced at Bryndan and away.

Trelk started to cry as he clutched his leg. Quand hauled the boy to his feet and began dragging him to the castle.

"Do you need a shyliac, Page Bryndan?"

Bryndan shook his head, still dazed. He rolled painfully to all fours, pausing to allow the dizziness to pass. His hand landed on a palm-sized rock. The arena was soft dirt, there shouldn't have been any rocks in it.

"Someone threw a rock?" His voice sounded hoarse. Bryndan couldn't make himself stand up just yet.

Jeo picked up the object in question, curious. "Is this what had him yowling like a cat caught in a tree?" He mused. He tossed the rock high in the air and caught it again. "That person has good aim—if they were aiming for his leg. A clever move, either way."

"Who threw it?" Bryndan croaked.

"Ah, therein lies the question." Jeo glanced at the crowd clustered around the arena. "Someone had a slingshot on the ready... but was it meant for Trelk, or yourself? Had you not fallen over your own feet," Bryndan flushed at Jeo's pointed comment, "it could have been you in that spot. Bent in half as you were, it might not have hit you in the leg as it did Trelk." Jeo clucked his tongue, thinking.

Trelk will fight dirty, Prince Damin's words came back to Bryndan.

Jeo reached out a hand and Bryndan allowed the instructor to pull him to his feet. Jeo tossed the rock into the air and caught it once more. He gave Bryndan a predatory smile.

"I shall very much enjoy tracking this person down," he said. "I think I'll start by having a few words with Trelk."

Jeo tossed the rock to the ground and nodded to Bryndan, then left the arena. Bryndan glanced over to the princess. She was beaming at him. Bryndan smiled back. She made him brave, he realized. He no longer felt intimidated by her. Perhaps, he would seek her out to talk to her. But not now.

Bryndan started to walk towards his friends, then hesitated. He scooped up the rock that had saved him and stuck it into a pocket. He had *won*. He thought he'd feel victorious for defeating Trelk. But he just felt sorry for the older boy.

Allec clapped him on the shoulder and Bryndan forced a smile. *You used to be the best of us*, Jeo had said. But he hadn't added the rest of that sentence: *before Leena died*.

For the first time in his life, Bryndan wondered if knighthood was something he wanted.

*   *   *

Taliya spun her staff around by her left shoulder. Her anger over what Trelk had tried to do to Bryndan in the arena earlier today gave her weapon an extra snap, and Damin whistled in appreciation.

"You know princess, I'm glad you're not a boy, else I fear I'd have a real competition," Damin said.

Taliya laughed at his teasing, trying to ease the tension in her shoulders. She had improved since he had started helping her, but she was still a kitten compared to him.

The moon had waned to a sliver and so Taliya had taken to bringing a lamp with her. As they practised, their shadows flickered over the bushes. The mornings continued to warm as the spring sun rose earlier each day.

Juliette had been commenting about the bags under Taliya's eyes, but Taliya had shrugged off her friend's questioning about where she went at night. Damin did not appear to be suffering from the lack of sleep. Or rather, he carried the same shadow with him as when they had met. It was the shadow of loss, and Taliya couldn't seem to touch it.

"I'll teach you the axyl dance soon. That will *really* test your skills… and your grace. Goodness knows you could use improvement on both."

Taliya swung at him and Damin grabbed the staff easily before it connected.

He stopped smiling. "I hear Prince Alastar is arriving sooner than he initially promised. He should be here before the Choosing Ceremony."

Taliya pretended she hadn't heard him and swung her staff around. She didn't want to think about her fiancé at all, in truth—especially not with Damin standing so close to her. She tried to pull her staff out of his grip, but he held on, staring at her. Taliya sighed.

"The letter arrived this morning. I'm surprised you heard about it already. Especially with all that excitement in the arena to focus on."

He gave her a smile that didn't reach his eyes. "You know me. I'm a bird in the wind. I hear everything." He paused. "How do you feel?"

Taliya stared at him, incredulous. "*How do I feel?* How do you *think* I feel? I haven't even met my betrothed, but as soon as my parents can arrange it, he'll be bundling me off to his country as his wife. I'll have no friends, no family. I'll be trapped with a heathen stranger in his home where my entire existence will be about bearing his children to carry on his line." She bit off the rest of her words and swallowed them down before they could turn into a sob.

Taliya stepped back, trying to pull her staff from Damin's grip, but he wouldn't let go, so she dropped her end of the staff. She wiped angry tears from her eyes and looked away. Damin abandoned the staves with a clatter and reached out to her. He cupped her cheek and turned her to face him.

Taliya shrugged; the fight had gone out of her. Her insides were all hollowed out. "It doesn't matter how I feel. I'll do what's expected of me. It's what I was born to do."

"Always the obedient princess."

Taliya clenched her fists. "*Don't*," she snarled, glaring up at him. "Don't you *dare* mock me. I thought that *you* of all people would understand."

"Taliya-"

"Go back to Glenifer, *obedient* prince. Go back and fight for your country. If you dare." Taliya turned from the hurt in Damin's eyes and stormed off. She wanted him to come after her and stop her. But he didn't. He left instead. Taliya leaned against a tree, listening to his footsteps fade away. She wanted to slap herself. Why had she said that to him? It had been cruel; it would serve her right if he hated her for it.

When she was sure Damin was gone, Taliya sought out Jef. She found him in the shed attached to the stables, meticulously cleaning his gardening tools. He stood and bowed when he saw her.

"Highness, what an unexpected honour." His words were clipped, distant. He had barely spoken to her since he had told her to stop training with Damin.

"Hello, Jef." She sank onto a bale of hay.

Jef returned to his cleaning. The silence stretched for a few minutes more.

"I quit," Taliya announced. She leaned against the wooden post and waited for his reply. She didn't really mean it, but she wanted to see how he would react. Long minutes stretched by.

"Perhaps it's for the best." Jef didn't ask what she was talking about.

"I doubt it." Taliya hugged herself. Her stomach churned with anxiety as she thought about the look in Damin's eyes when he had left her. Would he forgive her?

Taliya hadn't realized until then that it wasn't just the training that she had looked forward to; it was Damin's company. And she had ruined it. Already his absence made her chest ache.

She reached to twist her ring and wrung her hands awkwardly when she remembered it was gone. Its presence had always calmed her, and she wished that she hadn't given it up so foolishly. She thought of praying to Mother Jualis for its return, but it seemed near-blasphemous to bother Her with something so trivial.

Eventually, Taliya dragged herself over to say hello to Holjack. At least her horse was always happy to see her.

"It's getting late, Highness," Jef said.

Taliya sighed and trudged back up to the castle. She glanced back once to the stables, half hoping for a goodbye. But Jef didn't look up from his work. *He's not your friend,* she reminded

herself. *He's a servant. You don't care what he thinks of you.* Taliya
could almost believe it.

*   *   *

Taliya gave Bryndan a small smile when she entered the
tribunal chamber. He didn't smile back.

She paused, then took a seat near him. Her actions were not
unnoticed by the Council, and Lord Kade frowned at her. She
could almost hear his reprimand that she shouldn't choose
sides. But Taliya ignored him and stayed seated where she was.
She had no voice in the tribunal, but she could offer support to
her friend. She glanced over the people who would be deciding
Page Trelk's fate. Because it was a tribunal and not a Council, a
few of the members at the head table were different. Her cousin
Erok was there, as was Lord Kade. But the women were
replaced with a few knights and instead of the king it was
Sorcerer Craelyn who held the chair.

Trelk stood on one side of the room, with his father behind
him. Normally Trelk's father was part of the tribunal, but he
had been forced to step down today due to his conflict of
interest. Today, he would be representing his son.

Taliya glanced back to Bryndan to see if his father was
here—she had never met Bryndan's father—but he sat alone.
Normally witnesses were not permitted inside the chambers
unless they were giving Voice to their witness, but since
Bryndan was the main person who was harmed by Trelk's
actions, he could exercise the right to hear the tribunal in its
entirety rather than to enter just to give Voice. Obviously, he
had chosen to exercise that right today, although he didn't look
happy about it.

Someone sat down beside her and she turned her attention
away from Bryndan. Whatever was upsetting him, it was
obvious that she wasn't helping things by talking to him. She
glanced over to see who had sat beside her and saw Allec there.
He looked worried, too. Surely there was nothing to worry
about. The tribunal was fair and there *would* be punishment to
Page Trelk. Everyone had seen that he had tried to kill Bryndan.

Taliya turned her attention to the front of the room as Lord Kade called for order.

He said the usual blessings to the gods, then gestured for the first witness to be brought in.

Lord Jeo's testimony was succinct. He spoke not a word more than he had to in describing the events leading up to his decision of calling for the challenge, and the challenge itself. When he was done, he bowed and left the room.

Sir Quand came in next, but at his entry Trelk's father surged to his feet.

"What is this? We're allowing Imasdain to involve themselves with Kilaryan justice?"

"He speaks witness. As a visiting knight, he has Voice in this tribunal," Lord Kade said. Bryndan was picking at a thread on his trousers and not seeming to pay much attention to the tribunal, but she could see the tightness in his shoulders.

"Imasdain laws are *not* our own," Trelk's father sputtered. "We cannot rely on his testimony."

Taliya glanced at Sir Quand, whose face was bland. He looked straight ahead at the tribunal, his body posture relaxed, as if they were discussing nothing more interesting than the upcoming Spring Festival.

Lord Kade looked to the tribunal members. Despite the wizened age of many of the knights on the Council, all of them turned to Sorcerer Craelyn, who frowned.

"Sir Quand's testimony can have no more information than Lord Jeo's," he said slowly. "While he is a valued guest in our realm, he has no Voice in this tribunal."

Lord Kade turned to Sir Quand. "Dismissed, Sir Quand," he said.

The knight bowed and turned away. He did not seem perturbed, but Taliya blushed on his behalf. Did it hurt his pride to have his Voice refused by the tribunal? If it did, he did not show it.

Once he had left the room, Lord Kade called Trelk to the stand. Trelk's father stood in his son's place, and he spoke smoothly.

"As you all know, Trelk has suffered greatly this past year with the death of his beloved twin sister. Leena was a beautiful girl, and her laugh could bring light to the whole room." He glanced at the men on the tribunal. "But we are not here to talk about the hole that Leena's loss has left in our lives," he added hastily. "Was my son rash when he sought to seek out his own justice for Leena's untimely death? Perhaps misguided, but I respect his attempt to restore honour to his sister—Berech rest her soul."

Taliya scowled at the man. He spoke as if Trelk was guilty of a minor misdemeanour, not attempted murder of Bryndan, a fellow page.

Trelk's father sighed and wiped a tear from his eye. "I love my boy," he said in a voice that cracked. It was too perfect to be real and Taliya ungraciously wondered how long he had practiced the gesture in front of the mirror. "I love my boy as much as I loved my daughter. The punishment he has already suffered this past year is torment enough for him. He has learned from this mistake, and I assure the tribunal it won't happen again."

He looked at his own son, then Bryndan. "Berech knows," he said, turning his gaze to Lord Kade and Sorcerer Craelyn. "*We must protect* our *children*." Again, a furtive glance at Bryndan, but one with meaning.

Taliya blinked in surprise. The last part had sounded less like the compassionate speech of a grieving father, and more as if it were a threat. Sorcerer Craelyn and Lord Kade both stared at him, blank faced.

Not all the children are children. Lord Maddoux's words came back to her, and she looked at the faces of the tribunal. A few, like her cousin, looked confused, but others had adopted the same blank stare as Lord Kade and Sorcerer Craelyn. What did it mean?

As Taliya puzzled it through, Trelk's father nodded, and took his seat. Lord Kade looked to Bryndan.

"Have you a representative to speak on your behalf?" He asked, although the words were a formality. Everyone could see that Bryndan sat alone. Normally, the boys who couldn't have their fathers present at a tribunal were represented by the training master, Lord Jeo. But he could not give both witness and act as representative, and so Bryndan sat alone.

Lord Kade gestured for Bryndan to move to the speaking area. He slowly got to his feet and shuffled to the front, his head bowed and his shoulders tight.

"Speak your witness, page Bryndan. The tribunal will hear your Voice."

Bryndan cleared his throat twice, but even after he began talking, his voice still cracked. "Lord Jeo's witness was true, and I have nothing to add to it."

He bowed and sat back down in his spot. Taliya stared at him, willing him to say more. She knew the bullying had been worse than Lord Jeo had described, yet why did he hold his tongue? Why didn't he stand up to the tribunal and share his truths?

Lord Kade went to the Council and they whispered together for a few minutes. Sorcerer Craelyn did most of the talking.

Lord Kade returned to his spot and spoke to the audience. "The tribunal finds Page Trelk guilty of over-stepping his rights in the arena during the challenge, though we are not without compassion as to his reason. His punishment shall be as follows: from now until the Choosing Ceremony, he is not to be alone with Page Bryndan, nor are the two to spar together— either in training or outside of training. If Page Trelk is not chosen at the Choosing Ceremony, this ruling holds true for one year from today. If Page Trelk is chosen, his knight commander will be informed of this tribunal's decision and at that time any and all further disciplinary action or restraints will be at his knight commander's discretion, as per Kilaryan law. All are dismissed. May Berech guide your footsteps."

Taliya blinked, stunned. Was that it? It wasn't even a *punishment*.

Trelk smiled and hugged his father. They left in triumph, neither looking over at Bryndan. The tribunal slipped out their private exit at the front and the crowd filtered out slowly through the back of the room. There had been a lot of people in the room, most drawn here for gossip and entertainment.

Allec stayed beside her. When most of the people had left, Taliya leaned forward once again and put a hand on Bryndan's shoulder. He shrugged off her hand and walked out the room without a backwards glance, using the same front door that the tribunal members had used to avoid the crowds at the back.

She turned to Allec and gave him a helpless shrug. He frowned at her and rose stiffly to his feet. The crowd had mostly dissipated by this point, and when Taliya made moves to follow them down the main corridor, Allec gestured for her to wait. Once they were alone, he turned on her.

"You should have done something," he snapped.

"Done what?"

"You should have spoken up. Trelk tried to kill him, and he gets *no* punishment? What type of justice is that?"

"It's the Council's decision."

"So Kilaryan justice doesn't apply to the powerful?" Allec snarled.

"Allec, don't say that."

"How could you let them do this?"

"It's not my fault!"

"Why didn't you step in like you did after the forest incident? You looked out for us then—made sure Bryndan and I weren't banished from the castle. But here you did *nothing*."

"This is different. I requested Voice before Council because I had that right, but I can't interfere with the knight's tribunal! What could I do?" To her shame, she found tears of anger filling her eyes. He could not know how much that last comment stung, how much she longed to be valued—not as an Aminthian bride, but as Kilarya's Queen.

"The tribunal would've listened to you. Bryndan's your *friend*. Don't you even care enough to step in for what's right?" Allec's hands clenched and unclenched, as if he wanted to shake her.

Taliya flushed and narrowed her eyes. "And what *exactly* was I supposed to do, Page Allec?" she hissed. "I'm not on the Council. I wasn't a witness. What Voice could I have offered?"

"You're the crown princ-" Allec choked on his words and flushed.

"I'm *not* the crown princess. Not any more, Allec. You should speak to Milahny about your concerns. Or perhaps Erok."

She didn't wait for him to bow. She brushed past him and hurried on before he saw her cry. She bumped into Damin, who gave her a blank stare and Taliya wondered how much he had heard. He turned away before she could say anything. Tim did not meet her gaze as he went after his prince.

That night, Damin did not show up at training. Taliya waited for him until past dawn.

16

"Children are not the future. Rather, they bring the future with them." – Gleniferite proverb.

Bryndan glanced around him as he shut the door behind him and said a prayer to Sorcerer Maddoux 's spirit, praying that it wouldn't haunt him for what he was doing. After staring at the ceiling all night while sleep eluded him, Bryndan finally rose in the early hours before dawn so he could be alone and gather his thoughts.

He couldn't handle it right now. His friends who looked at him with open bewilderment, the servants who glanced at him discretely and pointed and whispered when they thought he couldn't see him, and the teachers who pressed their lips together but voiced nothing of their thoughts. But Bryndan knew. He *knew*. Every one of them hated him. Trelk was well liked by most of the teachers, and his father was very influential in the courts. Bryndan was the fourth son to a lowborn noble, and the only thing his family had ever done of note was when his older brother got Leena pregnant in that scandal. Asking Bryndan to speak his Voice in tribunal was a joke—nobody would hear him. Nobody would *want* to hear him. And, a small part of him whispered, he didn't deserve to be heard. Not after what his family had done to Leena.

Bryndan couldn't find an escape from the others. Even the gardens had servants who whispered and stared. But then a brilliant idea had struck him: Sorcerer Maddoux's chambers had remained empty since his passing. It wasn't forbidden for any to go there, but why would anyone bother?

As Bryndan slipped into the corridors leading to Sorcerer Maddoux's chambers, he knew his gamble had been correct. There was not a soul to be found. He glanced into a few rooms to confirm this and found to his satisfaction that the entire wing was empty. The door to enter the wing had been heavy and reluctant to open, and Bryndan had barely managed to squeeze in. He shut the door behind him with difficulty and sank down against a wall and closed his eyes; peace at last. They had cancelled Trelk's classes yesterday for the tribunal, and today was a day of rest, with no classes scheduled. Nobody would miss him right now.

Eventually, curiosity grew stronger and he stood up to look around. He had never been in a *sorcerer's* chambers before. Sorcerer's never used fosterlings as errand boys, and Bryndan hadn't been important enough to draw old Maddoux's attention. But what he remembered of the old man had been his gentleness. Surely such a kind soul wouldn't mind Bryndan looking around? He wouldn't touch anything, of course. Just a little peek, to see what a sorcerer's chambers looked like.

He opened a few doors that creaked loudly, and Bryndan winced at the noise. But as nobody was around to get him in trouble, he poked his head around each one. Most appeared to be empty. One room had a door that opened silently and easily. It appeared to be the sorcerer's work room. It was still filled with papers and books. There were a few chairs that looked used. Bryndan glanced at the papers but didn't touch them. They appeared to be symbols—code, Bryndan realized. And not one that he recognized.

There was a mantle at the far side of the room that was as tall as Bryndan, but it held no fireplace. It was odd and out of place enough that Bryndan went over to look at it. Carvings marked the border of the mantle, but nothing else interesting. While he was there he noticed that one of the bookcases next to the mantle was pulled out from the wall a little bit. Maybe there was a secret entrance past there. He squeezed into the space to see if he could find it, but he saw the reason for that was that another part of the wall jutted out a bit farther into the room.

Interestingly, he could see that the shelves of the bookcase didn't quite connect all the way to the top, which gave him a thin slit with which he could see the rest of the room. But since there was nobody to spy on, it was quite useless. Disappointed, Bryndan wiggled back out. In another year he wouldn't fit in that space at all.

He left the room and walked across the hall. *Just one more room.* He promised himself. *I'll just take a quick peek and then I'll leave.*

This room, like many of the others, was small. But it had manacles attached to the floor. He frowned at the manacles and took a closer look. They were small. So small, that when Bryndan held one up to his wrist, he realized it wouldn't fit even him, despite his size. For children? He shivered away from the thought and backed out of the room quickly and shut the door.

It was a mistake to come here.

He turned to leave, when he heard footsteps coming from down the corridor. The person grunted as they pushed on the heavy door that opened into the corridor. Bryndan's heart pounded and his mouth turned to sand. What would the person do if they caught him? It might not be expressly forbidden to visit Sorcerer Maddoux's chambers, but suddenly Bryndan didn't want to find out how much of a grey area it was.

He dashed into the office room and looked for a place to hide. He instinctively went to duck under the desk but stopped himself. If anyone sat on the desk they would see him instantly. He scurried over to the bookcase and squeezed himself back behind it just as Sorcerer Craelyn rounded the corner. The sorcerer was frowning as he looked around the room. Bryndan could barely breathe with terror.

"Anything wrong, Craelyn?" the king's voice asked and Bryndan's knees weakened. Sure enough, the sorcerer moved out of the way for the king to enter.

Sorcerer Craelyn shrugged but did not answer. His eyes were narrowed as he looked around the room.

Bryndan bit his lip hard. If it hadn't been forbidden to visit Sorcerer Maddoux's chambers, listening in on private Council between the king and the sorcerer was treason. But was it already too late? What if he spoke up *now*? Would this still be considered treason if the king found him hiding? Berech help him, he didn't know what to do.

Lord Kade entered the room as well, looking deeply unhappy. He crossed his arms and drummed his fingers.

"Let's get this over with," he gritted out.

The king sighed and dropped into the chair behind the desk. Thank Father Kilmar Bryndan had not chosen to hide under there!

Sorcerer Craelyn nodded sharply and turned towards the mantle. Bryndan stared at the sorcerer. Lord Kade and the king looked upset, but Sorcerer Craelyn looked... he looked... Bryndan swallowed. Sorcerer Craelyn looked *not* upset. Bryndan couldn't figure out the expression on his face. He couldn't understand what was going on.

"The village is about to be struck with a landslide. No survivors. These children will live. They will bring to us new life and hope," Craelyn said.

"We keep the rules," Lord Kade growled.

"We keep the rules," the king repeated, his voice hollow.

"We keep the rules," Sorcerer Craelyn repeated, licking his lips.

"Those that are bound to die," Lord Kade said, his fists clenching. "Those that are lives almost lost."

"We save them to bring them nigh." The king's shoulders sagged a little more. "To bring hope, no matter the cost."

It sounded like a vow, or an incantation. Bryndan's heart pounded in dread. What was happening? What village?

Sorcerer Craelyn bowed his head once in a salute to the two men, then strode over to Bryndan's bookcase. Bryndan cringed back, barely breathing. The sorcerer passed out of Bryndan's line of vision, but then to his right Bryndan saw the sorcerer's hands run across the runes on the mantle. They started glowing as the sorcerer muttered words, and the air pressure in the room increased until Bryndan's ears popped. A small wind came from the mantle and there was a high-pitched screeching noise that made Bryndan want to cover his ears, though he didn't dare move.

The sorcerer must have knelt, for his hands reached into the mantle from a lower level. The mantle no longer contained a wall of stone but a black emptiness that had wind coming out of it. He reached so far into the mantle that his face came into view, and Bryndan's heart skipped a beat. If the sorcerer turned his eyes to the right, he would see him. But Sorcerer Craelyn's eyes were staring into that dark abyss. Bryndan averted his gaze, lest the weight of it draw the sorcerer's attention.

From the corner of his eye, he saw the sorcerer pulling something from the mantle and fling it into the room. He did this again, and again twice more.

Bryndan looked to see what Sorcerer Craelyn had tossed into the room, and he felt bile in his throat. Children. The sorcerer had pulled in four children. Bryndan looked again to the mantle, but it appeared that Sorcerer Craelyn was closing it. The hands were running across the runes once more, and the blackness faded back into the wall. The wind stopped.

Knees trembling, Bryndan stared at the children in the room. He might not have been the brightest page in his class, but he wasn't born yesterday. He knew very well that there were parallel worlds out there and had heard rumours that some sorcerers had the power to cross them. But kidnapping children? What had they meant with their words about the rules?

The children were young—not a single one older than a toddler. None of them were conscious. Bryndan stared at them, wondering if they were dead. But then he saw the rise and fall of small chests.

"It is done," Sorcerer Craelyn said. He went and knelt beside the children and ran a hand over their sleeping forms. At first Bryndan thought it was out of compassion, but then he saw magic spilling out of his fingers as he brushed over each one. He stopped at a small girl.

"This one," he said. "This one might not be a child." He sounded annoyed.

The king rose to his feet, looking like it was an effort. "Are you sure?"

"Not entirely. But if she is one of the Guardians, I will be able to find out. If she is not, she will not remember anyway."

The king nodded, looking away. He reached down and gentle picked up two of the toddlers, and Lord Kade picked up one. He paused at the last child, but Sorcerer Craelyn put a hand protectively over the little girl to prevent Lord Kade from touching her.

"I will handle this."

Both the king and Lord Kade left with the three children. The sorcerer stood there a long time, staring at the little girl sleeping on the floor. Bryndan shivered as he waited.

Eventually, the sorcerer picked her up and carried her out of the room, using his foot to snag the door and shut it behind him. It was a long time before Bryndan had the courage to stumble out of the bookcase, and even longer before he found enough willpower to leave the room. As he slipped into the corridor, he stared at the door across the hall. Behind the door was a room that had manacles for children. He took one step towards the door when his courage drained away and he fled down the hallway. It took a minute to open the heavy door to the wing, but then he was free. He made it all the way out to the gardens before he vomited on the ground, shaking and shuddering. A few servants gave him curious looks, but none approached. He curled up into a ball and lay there, wishing he had never gone to Sorcerer Maddoux's chambers.

"Bryndan?" a voice whispered.

Bryndan curled into a tighter ball. The person dropped down beside him.

"Bryndan," Taliya said gently, and Bryndan jerked, letting out a small sob.

He peeked out at her, realizing that it was full dark.

"What-" he hiccoughed. "What are you doing here?"

"I was waiting for…" she hesitated and shrugged. "Never mind. Are you all right? Are you so very upset about Trelk's tribunal?"

She sounded sad. Bryndan almost laughed. He had forgotten all about Trelk. He sat up slowly, scrubbing his eyes.

"It's the children…" Bryndan trailed off. How much did she know? If her father knew about the children, surely she must know.

Taliya's eyes gleamed under the light of the lanterns.

"What about the children?" she asked in barely more than a breath.

Bryndan turned his head and scooted away from her. "Nothing. Never mind."

"Bryndan," Taliya said, her voice strained. "*Tell me* about the children. What is happening?"

"No, it's nothing."

Taliya took a deep breath. "*Not all the children are children.*"

Bryndan flinched and looked at her. She leaned forward until all he could see was her face. "Do you know what that means, Bryndan?"

"What do *you* think it means?" he asked.

Taliya rocked back on her heels, assessing him. "I don't know," she said finally. "It was something Sorcerer Maddoux said, before he died. Sorcerer Craelyn told me it was nothing but…" she frowned, looking in the distance. "Something is wrong. I *know* something is wrong, but nobody is telling me anything." This last was said almost to herself.

Bryndan's breath caught in his throat in hope. Maybe she *didn't* know about what the sorcerer was doing.

"Sorcerer Craelyn is lying. He's a part of it."

Taliya nodded as if she expected as much.

Bryndan cleared his throat, dreading what he had to tell her. "So was… so was Lord Kade and the king."

Taliya inhaled sharply. "My father has something to do with the children not being children?"

Bryndan started to nod, then shook his head. "Yes… no. Not exactly. It's hard to explain."

"Explain it to me, then." She commanded.

"I… I can't explain it."

Taliya gave him an assessing look. "You saw something?"

He nodded.

"Where did you see it? Tell me, and I'll go look myself."

"No," Bryndan said, surprising himself. "No, don't go alone." He took a deep breath. "I'll... I'll go with you."

Taliya nodded and stood up. She offered him a hand, but the thought of the princess helping him to his feet had him scrabbling up on his own. He dusted off his pants to hide his shaking hands, but she frowned, and he wondered if she'd noticed.

"Lead the way," Taliya said.

17

*"Who but a fool would question a sorcerer?" –
Aminthian Proverb*

Taliya followed Bryndan to Sorcerer Maddoux's chambers.
Her heart was pounding. Of course, *of course* it would be that
simple. In all her hours spent in the library and the temples,
never once had she returned to Sorcerer Maddoux's chambers
since his death. She had rarely visited this area of the castle even
when he was alive. It wasn't off-limits, exactly, but Taliya had
always had the strong sense that it wasn't exactly permitted,
either.

Bryndan grunted when he reached a heavy door and Taliya
helped him push it open. She frowned, trying to recall why she
had never noticed the door being heavy when Sorcerer
Maddoux was alive, then remembered it had always been left
open on the rare occasion when she sought him out in his
chambers.

She walked slowly down the corridor, feeling as if ghosts
were watching her. But they didn't stop in the sorcerer's old
bedroom. Instead, they went further down the hall. Taliya's skin
started to prickle.

Bryndan went to a door on the left, then hesitated and
glanced at her. The look on his face asked her, *Are you sure?*
Taliya nodded at him and he opened it and slipped inside.

Taliya slipped in after him and stopped in shock as she
stared inside.

Manacles. She hadn't known any room outside of the
dungeon to have manacles attached to the floors. Had Sorcerer
Maddoux questioned traitors in this room?

Bryndan was frowning at him, so she turned her attention to him.

He shook his head. "You're not seeing it."

"Seeing what?"

Bryndan knelt beside one of the pairs of manacles and held it up against his wrist. It was far too small for him to fit it around his wrist.

It took Taliya two heart beats to realize what it meant.

"For *children*?" she hissed.

He nodded. "Infants and babies."

She looked around the room and her heart ached. Surely Sorcerer Maddoux wouldn't have done this. And as she thought about it, she saw a difference in the stones where the manacles lay, and the stones on the walls of the room.

"Look," she said. "The stones with the manacles are newer. They haven't aged the same way."

Both examined the stones carefully.

"What do you think it means?" Bryndan asked.

"I think," Taliya said slowly. "I think it means these were installed *after* Sorcerer Maddoux passed into Father Kilmar's care."

Bryndan gave her a sharp look. "You think, or you hope?"

Taliya frowned, tracing her hand along where the manacles were embedded into the stone. She thought of the wizened old Sorcerer. He had always been so kind to her, even when she was small. And she remembered watching him as he soothed one of the servant's toddlers who had gotten separated from his mother. Taliya remembered thinking at the time that it was a shame that the Sorcerer's position didn't allow for a family.

"I know," Taliya said. "Sorcerer Maddoux *loved* children. He wouldn't have done anything to harm them." She looked at Bryndan. "This isn't all you found."

Bryndan stood up.

"I'll show you."

He led her out of the room across the hallway. Taliya wasn't sure she wanted to follow him. When he opened another door, Taliya glanced down the corridor and caught his sleeve.

"You could be in trouble for being here, if we're caught," she said. "If someone comes, I want you to hide. I'll lead them away from you as best I can. And no matter what, you stay hidden until it's safe. Okay?"

Bryndan frowned at her. "But what about you?"

Taliya waved off his concern. "None of them would punish *me*," she said, referring to her father, Lord Kade, and Sorcerer Craelyn. "And even if they were tempted, Prince Alastar will be here shortly to whisk me away to his castle where I won't be able to cause any more trouble here." Taliya tried to make it sound like a joke, but Bryndan's frown deepened into pity. He stared at her for a long, uncomfortable moment.

"All right," he said, leading her into the next chamber.

"Promise me," Taliya insisted.

"I promise."

She followed him into the next room, and her skin started to prickle even harder.

"I *know* this place," she whispered.

Bryndan barely glanced at her. "You visited Sorcerer Maddoux here?"

Taliya shook her head, here eyes drawn to the mantle with the runes over it. She traced the runes and looked at the stone wall underneath it. She reached out to touch the stones, then withdrew her hand, frightened.

"No, never. But I *know* this place. There is blackness here."

Bryndan nodded, distracted. "Sorcerer Craelyn called the blackness, somehow. And he pulled the children through."

Taliya stared at the stone wall beneath the mantle, and she felt as if she was staring into her nightmare.

Smoke filled the room, squeezing the breath from her lungs and making her nose and eyes water. The other Taliya was there, trapped, screaming her name. Taliya felt her hair catch fire and all bravery left her.

"Remember!" The other Taliya cried out. Taliya fled into the arms of the blackness.

"This is where I hid earlier," Bryndan was saying. Taliya drew in a raggedy breath and forced her thoughts back to the present. She stood up and looked at the bookcase Bryndan had squeezed behind.

"I couldn't fit in there," Taliya said, eyeing it. Bryndan squeezed back out.

"It's how I saw what happened. The king was sitting there, at the desk, and Sorcerer Craelyn was where you're standing at the mantle, when he did something that opened a door under the mantle. It was all dark, and he reached into it and pulled four infants through. The king and Lord Kade took three of them. Sorcerer Craelyn said the last one wasn't a child—that she might be something called a 'Guardian'—and took her. I don't know where they took them."

Taliya walked over to where the desk sat in the room and began looking at the papers.

"It's in code," Bryndan said.

Taliya nodded. "I know this code. Sorcerer Maddoux used to send me notes when I was a child. They were all written in code and I thought it was just a children's game he made up. But I guess it was real."

"Did he write it then?"

"Hmm?" Taliya asked, distracted. "Sorcerer Maddoux? No. This isn't his writing. I'm not as familiar with Sorcerer Craelyn's writing, but I know both my father's and Lord Kade's, and it is not theirs. I would guess that Sorcerer Craelyn wrote this." She pointed to the date at the top piece of paper. "See? This is from last week. There is nothing here from today. I guess it hasn't been written yet."

Taliya focused on the writings as she skimmed over paper after paper. She was vaguely aware of Bryndan shuffling nervously beside her, aware that she was taking too long, but she was desperate to learn what had happened here.

"Taliya," Bryndan hissed, tugging at her sleeve.

"Leave if you wish, Bryndan. I need to find out what happened here."

Bryndan made a noise in his throat and ran a hand through his hair, looking at the door. Taliya read through the papers. She pulled open the desk drawers until she found more and skimmed through those.

She clucked to herself, looking around the desk. When Taliya was younger, she was convinced she would find all the hidden rooms and passageways in the castle. Sorcerer Maddoux had caught her once and, instead of scolding her for it, he had joined her in the search.

"The key," he told her, "is to look at *what's different*. Is there a shallow wall when there shouldn't be? A draft with no source? By noticing what is different, you'll find what is missing."

Taliya opened the drawers and stared at them. One of them was less deep than the others. Smiling to herself, she explored that drawer until she found the hidden catch and pulled another notebook from the desk.

"The writing is different," Bryndan observed when Taliya opened the diary.

"It belongs to Sorcerer Maddoux." She scanned a few pages, her heart pounding as she noticed a pattern. Then she started flipping through the notebook to look at the dates, comparing them to Craelyn's notes.

"Look, here," she told Bryndan pointing to the date at the top.

"I can't read it," he reminded her.

"The date's not in code."

"I see it. But I don't understand why it's important."

Taliya's mouth went dry and she started to sweat.

"It-" she stopped as they both heard the groan of the door down the corridor.

Taliya surged to her feet. She threw some of the papers back in the desk and shut the drawers quickly. She shoved Sorcerer Maddoux's notebook into Bryndan's hands and hurried him over to the bookcase, pointing for him to hide. If it had worked as a hiding place before, it could work again.

Bryndan balked, staring at her with worry. Taliya shook her head at him. She mouthed *you promised* and pushed him again towards the bookcase. She turned towards the door and lifted her chin up as she heard Bryndan scrambling behind the bookcase. She clutched her skirts to hide her trembling hands.

The door opened. Taliya and Craelyn stared in shock at one another. The sorcerer was holding something in his hands, but Taliya was too distracted to see what it was.

"Princess. What-"

"Why are you covered in *blood*?" Taliya cut him off, her voice rising.

"What are you *doing* here?" Craelyn asked.

"Why are you covered in blood?"

"I don't answer to you."

"And *I* don't answer to *you*," Taliya retorted.

Craelyn sighed and went to a table behind the desk. He put the item he was holding and grabbed a cloth and poured some water from a pitcher onto it, then began wiping the blood off his hands and face.

"Whose blood is that?" Taliya demanded.

Craelyn paused, then continued rubbing the blood off him. He glanced at her, then turned his back to her and pulled off his tunic.

Blushing, Taliya looked away. He took a long time washing. Taliya wondered if he wasn't trying to make her uncomfortable so she would leave. But she wouldn't leave. *She wouldn't.* Not while Bryndan was trapped behind the bookcase.

Out of the corner of her eye she saw him grab the item he'd been holding and shake it open to reveal another tunic. He put it on over his head then turned to face her. Taliya looked back at him and eyed the new tunic. No blood on that one. He crumpled the bloody one and threw it into the corner.

He gave her a small, ironic smile and Taliya narrowed her eyes, crossing her hands over her chest.

"Not Kilaryan blood, I assure you. Not even human blood."

Taliya clutched a hand to her mouth in horror. "*Guardian* blood?" she squeaked, thinking about the infant Bryndan had told her about.

Craelyn frowned. "No, not Guardian blood either. Why would you think…"

He looked around the room, his gaze narrowed in thought. Then he looked back at her. "I have offered you my truth. Now pray tell, what are you doing here?"

Taliya swallowed bile that had risen to her throat as she stared at his hands. The blood was gone, but Taliya imagined she could still see it there.

"I am here to find answers."

He frowned at her. "Not the whole truth."

"Neither is *yours*. You haven't told me whose blood you had on you. What have you been killing, Sorcerer, to feed your spells?"

He didn't deny that killing creatures gave him power. Taliya knew there was a lot of magic to be gained if one could channel another creature's death. What she hadn't known was that Craelyn was one who did that. Had Sorcerer Maddoux ever…

Taliya cut off the thought. *Never*, she told herself fiercely. *He would* never *seek to gain from the death of another. He was a kind soul.*

"Let's just say that I have ridden Kilarya of a great evil today."

"What a busy day you've had, then," Taliya goaded him. "Kidnapping infants and killing evil."

He strode over to her and raised his hand to slap her. Taliya flinched back, but he only put a hand on her face and turned her to face him. He leaned down close so all she could see where his eyes.

"And how," he asked mildly, with the promise of threat in his voice, "would you know about *that*, I wonder."

Taliya stepped back, breaking from his grip. Had she given Bryndan away? Barely, she managed to prevent herself from looking behind her at the bookcase. She couldn't give away Bryndan's secret. He would be banished from the kingdom for sure, and possibly even executed for spying.

Another groan from down the hallway as the door was opened yet again, and Craelyn stepped back from her. They waited in silence while two footsteps came down the corridor.

"Taliya! Child, why are you here?" her father sputtered when he saw her.

Lord Kade put a hand on his brother's shoulder but said nothing.

"Why are you kidnapping children?"

"Oh, daughter. It's not what you think." Her father sank into the chair by the desk.

"Then tell me what it is. Are you killing the ones you think are Guardians?"

Lord Kade looked at the people in the room. Craelyn crossed his arms over his chest, looking surly, and her father looked as if he had the weight of a thousand sorrows on his shoulders.

Lord Kade stepped forward and offered Taliya a seat, but she shook her head.

"We would *never* kill children, Taliya. Even if they were Guardians." Lord Kade strode out of the room and returned a moment later with a girl in his arms. She was sleeping peacefully.

"You see? Craelyn thought she might be a Guardian, but here she is without a scratch on her."

Taliya reached out to touch her face.

"Will she be alright?"

"The children sleep for three days solid, and then they wake up with no memory of anything before they arrived. Some might remember a name, but most don't even remember that."

"What will happen to her?"

Lord Kade gently placed the little girl on some cushions in the corner of the room. She sighed and curled up into them.

"She'll be adopted into a family. They'll be told that her parents died and that she needs a family to raise her. We don't offer a reason as to how the parents died, and the families don't ask questions."

"Why would they not ask questions about her parents?"

"This is the secret of Eliva, Taliya," he told her gravely. "We're dying. There are fewer and fewer children who are born every year. Your father and I saw this when we were growing up. Too many couples were seeking out advice when they couldn't conceive children. And the midwives were called out day after day to attend miscarriages and stillborn births. It broke our father's heart to see this, but we didn't know what to do.

"Then, when Sorcerer Maddoux came into power, he saw a way for us to survive. He was able to breach a window between our world and the next. For years he had done so just to watch and learn from the other worlds, but sometimes the window he opened revealed a disaster in the other world—a flood or a fire—that would kill so many people. It broke his heart to watch, and he told the Council he was going to quit his spying because he didn't want to watch other people suffer. But then our father came up with an idea.

"Allandrex and I had just reached the age to join the Council when he brought us together to call for a vote. 'Our children are dying, and we won't survive if this continues. But in that other world they have too many people, and those people are being killed by disasters. What if we save them and bring them here?' The vote was unanimous in agreement. At first Maddoux saved everyone he could, but he quickly realized that only the toddlers and babies survived. The older ones couldn't survive the crossing between worlds. And if they did…they were so damaged when they got here that they would end their own lives within a month.

"So we met again as a Council. And this time, we set up rules. First, we would only take toddlers and babies. Second, we would only take them to save their lives."

Taliya hugged herself, looking at the mantle as she considered Lord Kade's words. "*I* was one of those infants, wasn't I? My nightmare about the fire… it wasn't a dream. It was real. You saved me from a fire."

Taliya hadn't realized her father had risen to his feet until she felt his arms go around her, hugging her in comfort.

"You are *my* daughter," he told her. "Nothing changes that."

Lord Kade came forward and put a hand on her shoulder.

"I was sick that one day when Sorcerer Maddoux called us to gather here." Lord Kade said quietly. "He monitored the other worlds daily, but he only called us on the occasion when there was a disaster."

Lord Kade exchanged a look with his brother.

"Your mother came instead," her father told her, continuing the tale. "Although the Council knew about what we were doing, it was only ever my father, Kade, and I who were with Maddoux when he brought the children across. But Kade was sick that one time and couldn't make it, and my father had already passed away. We needed another witness, and so your mother came." He looked down at Taliya and smiled, caressing her hair. "When she saw you—hair burned off and coughing on smoke—I think her heart melted. Every other child I'd seen was unconscious when they came through, but not you. You were struggling against Maddoux and screaming for your sister. It broke our hearts. We knew we couldn't give you away to someone else."

Taliya wrenched away from them. "*My sister?*" she asked, whirling to stare at the mantle. *"My sister died?"*

Mother Jualis help her, the other Taliya in her nightmare was *her sister.* Her sister who had died. Taliya swayed on her feet, but her father caught her up in his arms again.

"We couldn't save her, Taliya. We couldn't save everyone. Berech help me, your mother was traumatized at what she saw. I swore an oath that she would never have to face it again. She wanted—*we* wanted—to raise you as our own. To replace the family that you'd lost. And you're *ours,* Taliya. No matter where you come from, you are *our* daughter."

Shock coursed through Taliya's body, and she didn't know how to feel. Swept up in her father's arms, she had never felt so alone. She pulled herself from her father's grasp again, and he let her go.

"That's why I'm not on the Council. That's why I can't inherit the throne." Taliya's voice sounded distant, even to her. There was a buzzing sound in her ears that she couldn't shake, making her feel nauseous. Taliya swallowed the bile that burned her throat and started to cough when it went back down the wrong way. She spat out saliva, bending forward as she tried to draw breath through gut wrenching coughs and deep, shuddering sobs.

Nobody spoke as Taliya tried to calm her body down. Eventually, the coughing subsided, and her sobs turned to hiccoughs. Lord Kade offered her a handkerchief and she used it to wipe the snot and tears off her face. He also offered her a hand and Taliya realized that at some point she must have collapsed onto her knees.

She remembered that Bryndan was hidden in the room, watching all the drama unfold and her cheeks flamed in embarrassment. She turned to face the adults.

She caught Craelyn staring at her. In his face was both understanding and suspicion. She stared back at him, feeling her own suspicion rise.

"You said I was suffering from the fire when Sorcerer Maddoux rescued me. That you could see the effects of the fire."

The king nodded. Taliya pointed to the little girl. "Then what happened to *her*? You said it yourself, Lord Kade. *Not a scratch on her.* What disaster was *she* rescued from?"

Lord Kade and Allandrex stared at her, then turned their eyes to Craelyn.

His gaze was narrowed, and his hands twitched in rage. "*I* keep *the rules.*" He snarled.

Lord Kade frowned in thought.

"I read through the documents." Taliya gestured to the table. "Father said Sorcerer Maddoux looked through into the other world daily, but the dates on all his notes about taking the children are sporadic—once a month at most. And," Taliya said thoughtfully as she thought over what she'd read. "Every entry talks about what healing the children need to recover. *Your* notes, Sorcerer Craelyn, take place at least once a week, and I don't remember reading anything about what healings the children needed."

Craelyn stepped towards her, magic crackling in his fingers. "You read my notes?" he asked her darkly. "You *spied* on me?"

"Craelyn, you go too far. This is *my* daughter." Allandrex's voice held suppressed rage.

Lord Kade frowned and strode over to the table. He looked at the scattered notes, rubbing his beard thoughtfully. Craelyn looked between him and the king, and there was a bit of fear in his eyes.

Everyone was silent as Lord Kade looked through the papers. Eventually he looked up, his gaze fixed on the king.

"Sorcerer Maddoux was one of the greatest men I knew. He helped us save the children when he could. But not with such regularity. We would get a rushed message and arrive here to find him pulling them from a fire—or a flood—or another sort of disaster. Many of them didn't make it, and we wept with him over their little bodies. But Sorcerer Craelyn has been able to predict the disasters before they happen. I had been praising Berech that we could save the children before harm came to them. Perhaps I should have been questioning why."

"What are you saying?" Craelyn ground out, his voice barely above a whisper. Taliya shivered at the chill in it.

Lord Kade glanced at Craelyn, then looked back at his brother when he spoke, weighing each word carefully. "I'm saying that this last year has brought a lot of changes. Curious, that's all. We keep the rules, do we not? Perhaps… perhaps we should hold off on bringing through any more children for a while. We should first discuss these new changes with the Council."

"I am saving lives!" Craelyn snapped. "*Children's* lives. I keep the rules!"

Allandrex and Kade both frowned at him.

"You've not been accused of being an oath-breaker, Craelyn," Allandrex said. Taliya opened her mouth, but the look he gave her had her close it again. He gestured to the mantle.

"This stops now," he commanded. "We will discuss it at the next Council meeting."

Taliya looked down at the sleeping girl and went to pick her up. She was small and light in Taliya's arms.

"Where do they go?" she asked Lord Kade.

"Once they wake up, we have knights disperse them to different villagers. We have a list of families looking for more children—or any children—and we send them to those families. They're well looked after."

Taliya looked at her father. "Was I meant to be sent to a village as well?"

Allandrex gave a short nod. "Your mother, bless her, couldn't bare to be parted to you. The nobles have better medicine available and haven't had as much trouble conceiving thus far, so we've been sending the children to the villages to fill those gaps. You were one of two exceptions that didn't go to the villages."

"Who was the other?" Taliya asked sharply. If they had been raised as a noble, she might know them.

The king shook his head. "That is not for me to tell. Come, daughter. I'll show you where she can sleep. I think that is something we all need right now," he added pointedly.

Lord Kade and Craelyn both bowed and made to leave after them.

Taliya turned at the door to face Craelyn. His face was blank, but Taliya could see the rage in his eyes.

"Sorcerer Maddoux was wrong, and so were you," Taliya told him. She gathered the little girl closer in her arms. "*All* of the children are children. And we will protect them."

She didn't wait for his response, but followed her father out the door.

18

"Brawynns may be a cousin to the horse, but they could never be mistaken for one. Untrainable, vicious animals—a beast of nightmares. The only good brawynn is dead, and best killed on sight if you don't want to be eaten." - From 'Magical and Mythical Creatures', written by Lord Kade

Sir Quand strode through the dark gardens, heading for the training grounds. He heard the familiar murmuring of the two morning gardeners off to his right before he reached the outer gate. As usual, he was the second one on the field. It was almost pitch black; dark clouds covered the stars on the moonless night and only a tickle of sunlight could be seen. But Quand's eyes were sharp and he had no difficulty seeing.

Allec stood at attention before him, his eyes watering in the chilling breeze. He looked ready to fall asleep on the spot. The garden door opened again and more pages came stumbling out, followed by Lord Jeo, who had a savage grin on his face. The wind picked up even more.

As the boys lined up, the two knights inspected them under the pre-dawn light. Page Bryndan was still not present. Jeo had told Quand that they would give him until tomorrow to sulk about Trelk's tribunal, then they would hunt him down and drag him to his classes by the nose. To give him even that much leeway told Quand how outraged Jeo had been by the outcome. It wasn't an accident that Trelk was suddenly given extra tasks to do whenever he had free time.

Sir Quand had great respect for the Kilaryan instructor. Lord Jeo was renowned for turning out some of the best trained pages in Eliva. Quand examined them as he passed them.

Tension built up behind his eyes and he rubbed his forehead. A vision of midnight blue eyes burned into Quand's head, and he stumbled. Gods help him, the brawynns were close.

"Quand, are you all right?"

Quand looked towards Jeo, but he could only see those alien eyes, as if they were imprinted on his brain. The wind started to howl as it gathered strength.

"Brawynns," he grunted. "They're coming."

"Father Jualis help us," Jeo whispered. "Is it an attack?"

Quand gritted his teeth. He needed to get everyone to safety, but the pain was almost crippling. That would mean there were more brawynns gathered than he had ever faced before.

"The wind! They always bring the wind to hide their approach when they attack."

Jeo drew his sword and looked to the skies. He squeezed Quand's shoulder in trust even as he barked orders at the pages. "Everyone back to the castle! Eyes to the skies, lads. Let's stay together."

Quand sliced his palm with his sword and pressed it into the ground, offering his sacrifice to Eliva. The pain stopped immediately, although the vision stayed strong. He loathed bleeding like a rare steak before these beasts, but he needed to have a clear head. Kilmar take him before he ever showed weakness before a brawynn. Wide-eyed, the pages followed Jeo obediently. They hadn't gone far when Allec cried out.

"There, *there,*" he said, pointing to the sky behind them. Quand's heart leapt into his throat as he made out the large, carnivorous sky horses closing in. It was hard to tell how many there were in the strong winds. Jualis help them, the brawynns were too close.

Yames whimpered and broke into a run. Quand grabbed him by the arm and stopped him before he had gotten three steps.

"No! Run and they will kill you. Stay together, stick to my pace, and they may let us live." Quand didn't believe it. Not when everyone had their claws out for an attack. They were going to be slaughtered, but he couldn't admit that to the pages. He couldn't take away their hope.

"Bryndan!" Jeo yelled across the field. Quand looked over towards the gate and saw Bryndan jogging towards them. Trust the boy to return to training the very day they were under attack. The boy stuttered to a stop as he gaped up at the brawynns.

"Bryndan! Get back to the gardens. Now!"

Bryndan stumbled over his feet as he turned and ran.

"No!" Quand cried.

One of the winged beasts pulled away from the group and veered towards Bryndan. The claws of its front legs reached out towards the page and a mouth full of rows of razor-sharp teeth split into a repugnant grin.

"Bryndan, drop!" Jeo shouted, fighting to get his voice to carry above the wind.

Bryndan dropped, and the brawynn's sharp claws grabbed air instead of flesh. Its teeth clacked in outrage. Others swooped to join their comrade, circling Bryndan from above. One swooped down towards the page. It snagged his tunic, and Bryndan screamed as he was lifted from the ground. The cloth ripped, dropping him back to the earth with a thud. He put his hands over his head and curled into a ball. The brawynn howled shrilly, and the others clacked their teeth in approval.

"Berech save us, they're *playing* with him." Jeo gripped his sword tighter and quickened his pace across the field.

"Like a cat plays with a mouse," Quand agreed.

Another brawynn swooped down, this time clawing Bryndan's back. Bryndan screamed again.

Quand cursed. He would not sit by and watch the page be slaughtered. He broke into a run. "Don't run!" he commanded the others in the group.

Jeo let out a war cry and, ignoring his friend's orders, ran after Quand. The pages followed suit.

Allec shook his sword at the sky as he ran. "Come get us!" he taunted, trying to draw the brawynns away from Bryndan.

The brawynns that surrounded Bryndan turned towards the group and hissed. Bryndan took advantage of their distraction. Scrambling to his feet, he bolted the last few yards to the garden gate. A brawynn screamed in triumph as it dove down towards him, just as he started to haul the gate open. Quand was close, but the brawynn was faster.

Out of time, they were out of time.

Quand heaved his sword and threw it with all his might. It struck the monster in the wing. Not enough to cripple it, but enough that it faltered for a second. That second was all that Bryndan needed to slip inside to safety.

The brawynn turned on him with hatred in its eyes and hissed. Quand slowed to a standstill, and the others gathered around him as the brawynns circled and landed around them, effectively hemming them in.

"Follow my lead," Quand said. He knelt on the ground before the leader, his hands on his lap.

"Why?" Jeo murmured.

"They've landed. They only kill from the sky, which means that these ones are only going to hold us." He glanced up at Jeo, who still held his sword in a defensive stance. "Unless they think we're a threat, in which case they'll slaughter us all where we stand."

Jeo glanced around at the pages and nodded sharply. He placed his sword on the ground with the hilt facing the brawynn, then knelt beside Jeo. The pages did the same.

The brawynn that Quand had hit with his sword preened its damaged wing.

"Pity you missed," Jeo murmured, watching the injured brawynn.

"Meant to," Quand whispered back. "Blood begets blood with these beasts—it's the only law they know. The brawynns scratched Bryndan; I scratched one of them. Had I killed one, it would have killed one of us in return."

"You know a lot about them," Allec said quietly, eyeing them.

"Brawynn attacks are frequent in Imasdan, but it's usually only a family unit—three, maybe four brawynns. I've never seen so many in such a coordinated attack before." Quand glanced around. Outside of the eight that circled around them on the ground, at least a dozen more soared above them.

"What do we do now?" Allec asked.

"We wait. We are the hostages, I'm afraid. We must leave the powers of negotiation to our superiors."

19

"Elyan is no warrior. Elyan is a coward. But fear not, my children. I will return to you in the end. And I will save you all." – from the prophecies of Berech

Taliya stopped sparring with Damin and rubbed her temples as her head started to throb. It had been two days since she learned about the children. But with one question answered, a thousand more pounded through her mind. Who was she? Who was her sister? How could she be Elyan if she wasn't even from this world? What was her home world like? Taliya couldn't answer any of the questions, but when Damin reappeared in the garden last night to continue their training, he had brought with him a welcome peace. With him, she could focus on the present and let her other problems slip away. She couldn't bring herself to tell him about the children. It felt wrong to betray her father to him. Would he even understand?

Damin groaned and bent in two, grabbing his head. Midnight blue eyes appeared in her mind—the same eyes that she had seen when she had given up her ring in the woods.

"Drægons," Taliya whispered. "The brawynns are here."

Damin grabbed a knife from his belt and nicked his palm, then pressed both hands to the ground. Tim came running forward from the bush, his hand also bleeding.

Damin held out his hand for her and Taliya clutched her head as the ache intensified.

"We have to be quick," Damin said. "Trust me!"

Taliya gave Damin her hand. He pulled her down to a kneeling position.

"I'm going to cut your hand just a little. I need you to put both hands on the ground and say a prayer of offering."

"Who do I pray to?"

"Whichever god you believe in."

Taliya nodded and tried not to wince when he sliced her hand. He guided her hands to the ground.

Mother Jualis, let this work, Taliya prayed.

The blue eyes blinked at her and—although they didn't fade altogether—her headache cleared. Taliya felt as if she'd woken up from a long sleep—refreshed and rejuvenated.

"The brawynns are attacking," Damin yelled over the howling wind. "They bring the wind to hide their approach. We need to get to safety."

Taliya bit her lip. "The pages are outside today! We have to warn them."

"I'll go," Tim offered.

There was a scream from outside, and Taliya lunged forwards. Damin caught her arm.

"That was Bryndan!" Taliya cried.

She yanked on her arm to free herself, but Damin's grip was too strong.

"We *can't*. If they're under attack, he could be dead already. We need to get into the castle."

"But-"

Bryndan raced through the gardens.

"Bryndan!" Taliya cried in relief. Damin released her arm and she ran to him.

"Are you alright? You're bleeding!"

"Brawynns," Bryndan gasped. "We need help."

"My father will know what to do." Taliya lead the other three inside.

They surged past the servants, making their way to the castle wall nearest the garden, as they wanted to see if the other pages were safe. Bryndan hadn't known what had happened after he got inside the palace and Taliya's heart clenched as she thought of Allec and the others trapped outside or being slaughtered by the brawynns.

On the way up, she ran into her father.

"Taliya, what are you doing here?"

"We want to help."

He shook his head. "This is no place for you, Taliya. Stay inside where it's safe."

"Sir," Damin said. "I was part of the truce we made with the brawynns. If these ones came from Glenifer, they should know me. I can help."

Craelyn ran up behind them.

"Your Majesties, I'm here to-" He stopped dead in his tracks when he saw Taliya and her friends, and his lip curled a little at Damin. He offered her a curt bow to Taliya. Bryndan paled as he stared at the sorcerer and backed up until he stood behind Damin.

The king gave a brisk nod to Craelyn, then turned to Damin. "They are holding my people hostage," Allandrex said gravely. "Anything you can offer to return them safely is welcome. Come, stand with me."

Damin fisted his hand over his heart and gave a slight bow.

Taliya exchanged looks with Bryndan as her parents swept off with Damin, Tim, and Craelyn.

"Let's go," she said quietly, offering her hand.

Bryndan took her offered hand and together they followed the group to the castle wall. Once outside, Taliya and Bryndan kept well to the back to avoid all the bustling guards. Talon saw her and frowned, but he was calling orders nonstop and aside from a disapproving shake of his head, he didn't bother them.

"They're okay," Taliya whispered to Bryndan, looking down at the pages below. "See? They're all okay."

"So far," Bryndan whispered back. "But there's so many brawynns. They could kill them in less time than it takes to draw breath and we couldn't stop them."

"They won't kill them," Taliya said with more confidence than she felt. "My father will negotiate for their freedom."

One of the brawynns circled down from the sky, he beat his wings until the guards backed up and allowed him room to land.

He hissed at them and ruffled his feathers. When his feathers settled, so did the wind. Taliya hadn't realized how loud it had been until it died down.

"Who speaks for the murderers?" Its mouth was not designed for human words. It took Taliya a few heartbeats to translate its words in her mind into something intelligible. Every time it hit a consonant, its teeth ground together like a sharp nail on rocks, and all the *s* sounds came out as a hiss.

Allandrex stepped forward. "I am King-"

The brawynn drew itself up and clacked its teeth. Talon stepped forward until he was next to the king, but gestured to the guards to hold.

"We do not recognize you. We will only speak to one of *hers*." The brawynn shook its head like a horse. It surveyed the people on the walls.

"I am the king. No one else here has the authority to-"

"That one," the brawynn interrupted, using a claw to point at Taliya. "That one we recognize. We speak to the hatchling who is both yours and ours."

All eyes turned to Taliya, who swallowed hard. Craelyn eyed her suspiciously. What did they mean she belonged to them? Why were they choosing her?

Damin stepped forward and bowed to the brawynn.

"Do you know me?" he asked.

"Yes, Prince. You are far from your home."

Damin nodded. "True. We are all far from home today." He took a breath. "Blood begets blood, and brethren bows to brethren," he quoted. "I remind you that the laws of the brawynns allow for a neutral third party during negotiations. Allow me to be that neutral party, as representative of a land where the brawynns and humans live in truce."

The brawynn clacked its teeth while it considered. "Accepted," the brawynn said. It crowed into the air, and the other brawynns crowed back. Taliya shivered.

Damin turned to her and gravely held out his arm.

Allandrex stepped protectively between them. "No! We will do this *my* way."

"Father," Taliya put a hand on his shoulder. "We'll be fine, *trust* me."

"I won't."

"Father, look at our people on the ground. They trust us to help them. Let me help them. *Please.*"

Allandrex's shoulders sank. "You stay," he said to the one who was on the wall. "You stay as *our* insurance that no harm comes to mine."

The brawynn clacked its teeth. "I am the only one who speaks Kilaryan. My brethren will stay for me."

"We stay in the field." Damin pointed to the far corner. "There. No arrow will reach that far, but we can be observed by others. Your brethren can stay in the garden below. *And* you let the other hostages go immediately."

Taliya looked at Damin in confusion. Stay in the field? She was about to ask him what he meant, when the brawynn on the wall reached under its wing and pulled out some bundled rope. As it used its claws to open up the rope, Taliya saw it was a net. She flinched back.

"I'm not flying in that thing!" She hissed at Damin.

Damin turned to her. "I swear, it's safe. The brawynns never negotiate in front of others. They need to take us someplace away from the hostilities. No brawynn can lie, and it is against their law to harm negotiators. The only way you will come to harm is if someone hurts the brawynn in the garden."

"That will never happen," Talon said darkly. "I'll make sure of it."

"And I as well," Tim swore.

Taliya squeezed Bryndan's hand and released it, kissed her father on the cheek, then stepped forward with Damin into the net. Damin showed her how to sit so she was secure, and she wondered how many times *he* had ridden in this net before. Below her, she could see the pages and two knights stand and walk quickly inside the gate. If she did nothing else today, she had saved them.

Her stomach lurched as they took off and she gripped the net with all her might. The brawynn struggled under their weight for a moment, then he shifted his wings to catch the wind—which was picking up again—and settled into his rhythm. The air was cold and Taliya shivered, leaning against Damin.

"Open your eyes," Damin said.

Taliya shook her head.

"Taliya, you are one of the few people in the world who will fly with a brawynn. Enjoy this moment."

Taliya reluctantly opened her eyes and looked around. She squeaked when she saw the ground so far below, but then noticed that she could see the tops of the trees stretching out in the distance.

"Oh, *wow*. I can see the whole forest from here."

Damin laughed. "It's too big for that, but it is a pretty view. Hold on, we're going down. When the brawynn gets close to the ground he will drop the net, so you may get a bruise if you're not careful."

Taliya shivered. "The woods don't look so frightening from up here."

Damin cocked an eyebrow at her but didn't respond. The brawynn dropped the net gracefully when they had landed. Taliya looked back and saw that they were at the edge of the field, as promised. She could walk back to the castle in less than half an hour.

Damin helped Taliya to her feet and she shook out her skirts. Dresses were *not* the best thing to wear when riding in a net.

The brawynn turned to her, its gaze assessing.

"What did you mean when you said I was 'one of hers'?" she asked.

The brawynn stared at her. "You offered yourself to the drægonelle and she accepted. Now you belong to her. You will help us find her murderer."

"The drægonelle?" Taliya asked, finding more questions than answers.

"Our leader."

"The blue eyes, Taliya. Didn't you see them just before the brawynns came? Those are *her* eyes. The drægonelle is the leader of all the magical creatures."

She had offered her ring to those blue eyes, back in the woods. Was that what the brawynn meant? That by giving her ring to the drægonelle she had become a… a *subject*?

One of hers, it had said. Taliya didn't know how she felt about that.

"I don't know her," Taliya lied.

The brawynn screeched so loudly that Taliya and Damin clapped their hands over their ears. It dragged its claws into the ground and threw its head around like a stallion about to fight.

"Taliya," Damin spoke quickly. "I should warn you that just as the brawynns cannot lie, they can sense lies in those around them. I don't recommend you go down this path, as they take the truth *very* seriously."

She turned to Damin. "Since when do *you* know so much?"

Damin spread out his hands in a calming gesture. "I told you. My people have been negotiating with the brawynns for ages. Ever since I was a child I learned as much as I could about them, and by extent, the rest of the magical creatures. I've been involved with the negotiations since I was a squire."

Taliya shook her head. She was here to negotiate a peace with the brawynns, not chat with Damin about their politics.

"I apologize," she told the brawynn. "What I should have said was that I didn't know it was her that I'd met before. I'm sorry for her death, but what exactly do you want from us?"

"The drægonelle has been murdered by one of yours. We felt the murderer's power as it consumed her. You will find that one and serve it to us to meet our justice."

"When did this happen?"

The brawynn clacked its beak. "Three suns before this one."

"Three days ago," Damin translated quietly.

Taliya bit her lip as she calculated it out. Three days ago had been when Bryndan had shown her Sorcerer Maddoux's chambers. Her heart went cold as she remembered Craelyn coming into the room. She remembered what he had told her after she asked him why he was covered in blood.

"Let's just say that I have ridden Kilarya of a great evil today."

Taliya bit her lip. He hadn't told her who—or what—he had killed. But even if it had been him, could she give him up to the brawynns? Could she sign over his life so easily? As angry as she was with him for what he had done to the children, he was still Kilaryan. And to blame him would be to also blame her father, and Lord Kade, and Sorcerer Maddoux. One didn't stay angry at the dead.

"Do you know who it is?" Taliya asked the brawynn, stalling for time. She didn't *know* it was Craelyn. All she knew was that he had been covered in blood three days ago. But it could have been anything that he killed. And surely killing the leader of the drægons was worth boasting about? Surely that would have been news whispered among everyone in the palace?

"It is one who lies in your nest."

"They live in the castle," Damin translated.

"We followed its stink until we came upon your nest, but its stink is everywhere in there, and we don't know which of you it was."

Kilmar help her, it *had* to be Craelyn. Had he known what he was doing? Why hadn't he *said* anything to them when they were up on the wall? Or maybe he had already spoken to her parents about it, and Taliya just hadn't been informed. Gods, what if her parents had ordered the kill? Would they have guessed the repercussions?

"What will we get if we give this murderer to you?"

The brawynn drew its nails across the field, leaving deep gouges. "Peace," it said.

Taliya drew herself up. "You speak of murder and ask for peace."

"Blood begets blood. The murderer or the leader. We will take either."

They meant her father. If she didn't give up Craelyn, they would kill her father. But the sorcerer was too powerful for her. It's not like Craelyn would willingly walk over to the brawynns and allow them to kill him. And even if he did, the Council—her parents—would never agree to giving up Kilarya's sorcerer. Should the brawynns kill him, it would be an act of war.

Taliya rubbed her empty ring finger as she thought furiously. The brawynns could have massacred all of the pages and many more before they could be stopped by the knights—if they could be stopped. Taliya didn't know much about history, but her instincts told her that if it came to war, both sides would lose heavily. Taliya's heart rate picked up and she found it hard to draw breath. Gods, was there anything she could do that wouldn't lead her people to slaughter?

"Taliya," Damin said. "Taliya, look at me." He grabbed her by the shoulders. "It's okay. Calm down and take a deep breath, you've got this."

Taliya looked at him, and saw the trust he had in her. She grabbed onto that trust like a lifeline. She could do this.

"Your people came from very far," Taliya said. "Damin said you are far from home. Where did you come from?"

The brawynn ducked its head and seemed reluctant to answer. Finally, it said, "Glenifer," in a long hissing breath.

"Glenifer is in the midst of a civil war, and could be for many more years. Prince Damin is the last of his family, and he came here as a refugee, seeking help."

Damin frowned at her and crossed his arms. He did not appear happy with the information she was disclosing to the brawynn, but it wasn't a great secret.

"I don't know-" *who the murderer is.* Taliya bit off the rest of the sentence before she could say it. She couldn't tell them that she knew who it was; they wouldn't rest until they had killed him. And if she told them she didn't know who it was they would sense the lie. "-if it will be safe for you to continue living in Glenifer," she finished instead. She swallowed hard, trying to think of the proper way to say it.

"I know you have already started moving in to Kilarya, but the peace with the villagers will not last long unless it is decreed by the king."

"Blood begets blood. We will kill any who attack us."

"Of course, but wouldn't it be better if humans didn't attack you in the first place?"

The brawynn cocked its head, considering her. "Continue," it told her.

Taliya took a deep breath. "I propose—as an apology for this murder—that the brawynns be welcomed back to Kilarya to make this their temporary home until peace and stability is restored in Glenifer. The king will send out an announcement to all that brawynns are not to be harmed—unless they are acting in defence, of course."

The brawynn blinked at her, appearing confused. *Blood begets blood*, Damin had said. Taliya didn't know if the brawynn would accept a home—and a temporary one at that—over the sorcerer's blood, but she crossed her fingers behind her back for luck.

"Explain," it said.

"Give us one month to spread the word to all Kilaryans that you are to be welcomed in our land and not harmed. After that, you can move here and live in safety until your home is no longer in danger."

The brawynn shook out its wings in consideration. Finally, it said. "By the laws of brethren bows to brethren. Terms of contract: in one month, all brawynns of Glenifer will move to Kilarya. No human will raise harm against brawynns except in terms of blood begets blood. When human war has ended in Glenifer, brawynns that choose to return will return. Brawynns that choose to stay will stay. By that time, you will give us the drægonelle's murderer to mete out the justice of the brawynns, or contract broken."

"No. We offer you a safe place to live as apology for your drægonelle's death. I said nothing about giving you someone to kill."

It drew its head close to her, its breath smelling of rot. Taliya steeled herself not to step away, or gag.

"Blood begets blood," it hissed. "Terms of contract. Final. Or we return to Glenifer with head of your leader by next sun."

Taliya groaned inwardly. If she agreed to what the brawynn said, all she was doing was delaying the inevitable. But maybe things would have changed by then. Maybe she could work with her family and the Council to figure something else out. Or maybe Prince Alastar would have come to whisk her away by then and leave the others to clean up the mess she was putting them all in.

She turned to Damin, hoping he had some advice, but he remained silent. *Neutral third party* he had called himself. The negotiations were up to her. Taliya sent up a silent prayer to Mother Jualis and Father Kilmar that she was doing the right thing. Then she unclenched her hands and swept a graceful curtsy.

"I agree to your terms, on behalf of Kilarya."

"Witnessed," Damin said.

"Agreed," the brawynn said.

The brawynn turned to Damin and eyed him closely. "You are blind here. Would you like to see again?"

Damin inhaled sharply.

"What does he mean?" Taliya asked.

Damin didn't look at her, but instead nodded to the brawynn and closed his eyes. The brawynn reached forward and opened its mouth to reveal sharp teeth.

"Don't!" Taliya cried.

The brawynn lunged forwards and licked Damin across the forehead, then stepped back. Damin swayed and his face tightened, but after a moment he opened his eyes again and blinked like someone stepping into the sun.

"What was that?" Taliya demanded.

Damin's voice sounded far away. "I'm magic-sensitive, Taliya. The magic of Kilarya has been affecting me, and the brawynn offered to cancel it out… to protect me from it."

"They can do that?" Taliya asked with interest. Could they protect her from Craelyn's magic?

"It will work a few days at most," the brawynn said, sounding satisfied.

"Could you do that with me?" Taliya asked.

The brawynn cocked its head at her. It squinted its eyes to examine her.

"No."

"Why not?"

"You are not magic. You are lies."

"What do you mean?" Taliya crossed her arms to hide her shiver.

The brawynn ruffled its feathers in what could have been a shrug. "You are not magic. You are lies."

Taliya sighed. She doubted it would say anything more than that.

Damin was a little shaky on his feet from what the brawynn had done to him, so Taliya took his hand and led him back to the net. The brawynn scooped up the net and took off with help from the wind. Taliya's stomach lurched, but she felt giddy with relief and laughed out loud. She had done it. *She* had done it. Nobody else could have negotiated with the brawynns but her, and she had saved them—for the moment—from war. Her people wouldn't be happy to be ordered to let the brawynns back into the country, but at least they would be alive to complain.

Damin glanced at her and smiled. "Not bad for your first negotiation. I imagine there will be more in your future."

Taliya smiled back. "Jualis help me, I hope not!" she giggled, giddy with relief.

"Taliya," Damin said. Taliya glanced over. "Don't tell the others, please? About my being magic-sensitive."

"Why? It's not illegal."

Damin shrugged. "I just... I don't want anyone to know."

"Of course." She paused. "It's how you escaped from Glenifer, isn't it? Before you were killed?"

He nodded. "I could feel something dark coming towards me, and it had the taste of my bastard brother in it. I don't know how, but I managed to block it and hide. That's when Tim found me."

"Your secret is mine," Taliya promised.

She squinted up at the sky, where it appeared that the brawynns were in a skirmish of some sort. It reminded Taliya of when she had been riding through the village with her guard and seen a mob.

"What are they doing?" she asked Damin.

His eyes widened and his mouth tightened. He looked back at the castle and set his shoulders.

"Damin?" she asked.

Before he could answer, they were at the castle wall. The brawynn dropped the net and shook it, so that Taliya landed onto Damin in a heap. She flushed in embarrassment as he helped her back to her feet.

The brawynn that they had spoken with glided away to join the others. Taliya looked at the guards. Something was very, very wrong. Three of them were wiping their mouths and there was vomit on the ground before them. All of them looked sick and horrified.

"What happened?" she demanded.

Damin grabbed her hands. "We need to get downstairs, *now*." He yanked her forward and Taliya sprinted to keep up, his earlier shakiness evidently gone.

"Damin, Damin what is it?" Taliya was close to tears.

They raced out to the garden and found Talon, Tim, her parents, Bryndan and a few others gathered around a clearing. Damin shoved through them and Taliya followed.

"Taliya!" Bryndan saw her first. The others turned.

"Oh, praise Berech!" her mother said. "We feared the worst!"

The queen swept her up in a hug and her father followed shortly, his eyes wet with unshed tears.

Taliya peered over their shoulders to see what lay behind them. A brawynn lay there—it was the one that had offered to give itself up as hostage during the negotiations. It was dead.

"No!" Taliya cried.

Craelyn stood up from where he'd been crouching next to the beast, examining it with a stick.

"What have you done?" she cried.

"You're safe, Taliya. That's what's important," the king reassured her.

"How did this happen?" Damin asked, his voice thick with the promise of violence.

Craelyn dropped his stick and readjusted his cuffs as if nothing was amiss. "I was setting up defenses on the perimeter after you left. These beasts got past me once and I had to make certain it wouldn't happen again." He shrugged. "Had I realized the magic I used was strong enough to kill one of the beasts, of course I wouldn't have used it while you were at risk."

Taliya looked at him, and her whole body went cold. He was lying; he had known he would kill the brawynn. And by law of the brawynns, her life would have been forfeit; hers, or Damin's. Who had Craelyn been trying to kill?

"We agreed to it, Taliya," her father said. "We didn't know it would put you at risk."

She pulled away from her parents, her heart turning as cold as her skin.

"You *idiot*." She snarled at Craelyn. "Damin said the brawynns don't do well with human magic! How could you not have known?"

Craelyn held out his hands. It might have been an apologetic gesture, but Taliya saw the mockery behind it. He watched her with hooded eyes and a tight mouth that might have been suppressing a smirk.

"An honest mistake, Princess. And, of course, one I regret deeply."

Liar.

Her parents stepped back to his side, showing their support. *How could they have believed him? How can they still believe him? Do they know that he killed the drægonelle—that he was responsible for everything that happened today?*

"But she's fine," Damin said, stepping forward. "The brawynns didn't hurt her. It didn't hurt either of us. So who was it?"

It took Taliya a second to realize what Damin was saying. *Blood begets blood.* The brawynns would have killed someone in revenge for the death of their own. It wasn't Taliya; someone had sacrificed themselves to keep her safe. She clapped a hand to her mouth in horror. The brawynns in the sky hadn't been fighting each other, as she had presumed; they had been tearing some poor person apart. That's what Damin had known; they hadn't been looking at a mob, but a feeding frenzy. She staggered to a bush and vomited.

Bryndan's face was streaked with tears and both Tim and Talon looked white with shock. She looked around at the others in the garden—mostly knights and Council members. All of them cringed and looked away under her regard.

Taliya wiped her mouth with her sleeve as Craelyn shrugged. "Some gardener. As soon as we saw the brawynn was dead he went running outside and offered himself to them. I'm afraid they killed him before anyone else knew what was happening."

A sob burst from Taliya's mouth and she fell to her knees. "No! It can't be." Before anyone could react, she sprang to her feet and ran further into the gardens, searching frantically for Jef and shouting his name. He would be in his favourite spot, near the lilies. He *wouldn't* have gone out there. He would be-

Taliya saw his spade on the ground, and she knew. She grabbed the tool and screamed at the sky. She didn't know the others had followed until Damin caught her in his arms.

"It's okay, it's okay," he whispered to her, holding her and rocking her. "He was a brave man. He wanted to help you."

"Yes, that poor gardener," Craelyn said, his voice empty of emotion.

Taliya turned on him and lunged, holding the spade like a sword that she could slice through the sorcerer's heart.

"I'll kill you!" she screamed at him. "I'll kill you!"

Craelyn offered her a small smile and bowed sardonically. "It was a terrible accident that occurred, Princess Taliya. But I'm so glad you're safe."

"You killed him," Taliya choked out. "And I will kill *you* for this, Craelyn, if I don't let the brawynns do it first."

"Taliya!" the queen said severely. "I know you're upset, but that's no way to speak to Sorcerer Craelyn. He was only trying to help."

Taliya never took her gaze from the sorcerer. After a moment, the amused expression disappeared from his eyes and

his face darkened in anger. "I won't ask you for an apology right away, as I can see you're upset. But you *will* apologize for your words before the week is out."

He turned and stalked away. Her parents shook their heads at her in disappointment and followed him, gesturing for the court and the guards to follow. Bryndan, Tim, and Talon hovered around, looking at her with pity. Taliya watched the rest leave, her whole body shaking. The spade dropped from her numbed hands as she felt her heart shatter into a thousand pieces.

20

"We leave you on your own now, our children. But just because we choose not to interfere does not mean that we do not love you, that we do not watch you always. We give to you this world and we give to you freedom to make of it what you will."
– From the book of Light and Life.

Eventually, they all left her to her grief. Damin had tried to stay, but she couldn't bring herself to look at him, and shuddered when he touched her shoulder. He was the last to withdraw. Only when he was gone did Taliya realize that one person had stayed behind.

Bryndan sat down beside her, saying nothing. They sat in silence as the sun crossed the sky and dusk settled around them.

"He loved his lilies," Taliya whispered hoarsely.

Bryndan nodded. "We should plant some. Right here. I think he'd like that."

"He's dead," Taliya said darkly. "He won't care."

Bryndan was silent for a long moment. "But *you* would care, and I care. It's about what we need to bring us peace. And if this Jef was alive right now, I bet that's what he would want."

"Peace is a dream," Taliya said, thinking about the brawynns. The clock was ticking. She had one month to figure out what to do. Knowing that Craelyn had caused this—had deliberately tried to get her killed—was making the decision seem awfully easy.

"He tried to get you killed," Bryndan whispered, voicing her thoughts. Taliya gave him a sideways look.

"Do you believe that?" she asked.

"Yes," Bryndan said with conviction. "I *saw* him in that room. When he first came in, he dismissed you. He didn't seem to care about you one way or the other. But then the king told you how you had been one of the children brought over, and his face *changed*. He stared at you as if you were a cockroach he wanted to kill. As if you were his greatest enemy. Do you think…" Bryndan stopped speaking and plucked at the grass.

"Do I think what?"

Bryndan shrugged. "It's just a silly theory, but… Sorcerer Craelyn said he was looking for something called 'Guardians.' That little girl you saw was one that he was testing for it. I got the feeling that Sorcerer Craelyn thinks being a Guardian is not a good thing."

"He called them destroyers," Taliya said, remembering his words when Sorcerer Maddoux had been dying.

Bryndan started and stared at her. "*Destroyers?* Gods, you don't look-" he cut himself off and began plucking at the grass once more.

"Like I'm a destroyer?" Taliya finished for him, forcing herself to smile.

Bryndan shook his head. "You're not evil, Taliya. I saw evil in that room, and it wasn't you. Maybe Sorcerer Craelyn's just worried because he thinks you're one of those Guardians. And maybe," he said slowly, "if you *are* one of them, it's a good thing."

"It's a good thing to be a destroyer?" Taliya asked mockingly.

Bryndan shook his head again. "To change something, you have to destroy what was. And you changed something, didn't you? Because of you there will be no more children brought over from the other world. At least, not for a little while. And that's a good thing."

"Is it?"

"Yes," Bryndan said with conviction. "What they were doing was wrong, no matter how they tried to pretend it wasn't."

Taliya wasn't so sure. The issue wasn't as black and white as Bryndan was painting it. But he was right—she had put a halt to it, at least for a little while.

They sat in silence for a while.

"So, do *you* think I'm a Guardian?" she asked lightly, trying to pretend that his answer didn't matter to her.

Bryndan thought about it for a few minutes, picking at the grass. "I think that you're *you*. Putting a name to it doesn't matter."

"And what if I told you I was Elyan?" The words came out before Taliya could stop them.

Instead of laughing, Bryndan considered her question.

"It would mean we're in for an awful time ahead if the world is ending. But if Lord Kade spoke truly, and the human race is dying… maybe the world had already started ending years ago. We just didn't know it yet."

That was a terrifying thought.

"And what would you do about it, if you were Elyan?"

Again, Bryndan considered her question carefully.

"I don't know," he said finally.

He stood up slowly and stretched, then reached down to offer his hand. Taliya looked at his hand but didn't take it.

"Let me help you, Taliya."

Taliya looked up at her friend, seeing in his face the unspoken promise to his words. His gesture reminded Taliya of the fire—when her sister had reached out to her for help and Taliya had turned from her to flee. But she wasn't a little girl anymore.

She put her hand in his and let him help her to her feet.

"Let me help you," he said again, his voice a whisper.

Taliya looked around the garden and shivered at the emptiness. She turned back to her friend.

"I would like that," she told him.

Hand in hand, they walked back into the castle.

About the Author

Laura lives in Alberta, Canada with her family, although she might argue that she splits her time between Alberta and the world of Eliva. When she was 11 years old, she went in search of her perfect fantasy book but - not finding it - she wrote it for herself. Obviously, it has gone through some changes since then, much as she has. When not working, spending time with her family, reading, or hiking in the Rocky Mountains, she is working on the next book. It is coming, she promises!

You can check out more stuff at **www.lauraziegler.ca**

Manufactured by Amazon.ca
Bolton, ON